OPERATION UMANAQ

D1632572

After near bisection at the delicate hand of his ex-girlfriend and an all-stations call from the head of his own security unit labelling him an outlaw, Mark Chevron was a two-time loser. And he had a tenuous line on the biggest operation ever mounted on the face of the Earth, with every man's hand turned against him.

Crossing two continents and reaching deep into the permafrost of Polar Scientific Complex, he is thrown into the middle of a war waged with one of the strangest weapons in man's history – ICE!

Other books by John Rankine

BINARY Z
INTERSTELLAR TWO-FIVE
MOONS OF TRIOPUS
NEVER THE SAME DOOR
ONE IS ONE
WEISMAN EXPERIMENT
THE FINGALNAN CONSPIRACY

Operation Umanaq

Science Fiction

by

JOHN RANKINE

SIDGWICK & JACKSON
LONDON

First published in Great Britain in 1974

Originally published in the U.S.A. by
Ace Books in 1973

Copyright © 1973 John Rankine

ISBN 0 283 98149 0

Printed in Great Britain by
The Garden City Press Limited
Letchworth, Hertfordshire SG6 1JS
for Sidgwick and Jackson Limited
1 Tavistock Chambers, Bloomsbury Way
London WC1A 2SG

I

AN URGENT bleep on orchestral A, hitting a harmonic of pulse rhythm, had Mark Chevron out of his deep foam sack reaching for his equipment belt in a count of three. He had moved halfway to the hatch, kicking himself into some kind of life before he was fully oriented to his current position in space and time.

Except for the gymbol-mounted bed and the brilliance of the stars through the curved observation port, he could have been in any small functional hotel room, but a glowing panel beside the door reminded him that outside was different in some key respects.

It said baldly *Life Support System* and punched the message home with a small picture of a man in full space gear for the benefit of any nonreaders who might have strayed onto the set.

Chevron veered off to the left, whipped open a locker and in ten seconds of concentrated effort converted himself into a bulky zombie.

As the self-sealing casque snapped shut he was isolated in his own personal acoustic shell, and the bleeps cut off until he had switched in for sound. Then they were back, amplified if anything, and somehow more urgent—as though they were beamed personally to him.

Recall was total. He was where he had been for the last week, on Satellite N5, which was holding its carefully judged course along the fifth parallel, marking a fellow traveler on the other side of the equatorial line and watching the interests of Northern Hemisphere Government with unsleeping zeal.

Also the bitter question mark was still there. As an

assignment for a top rank operator, this mission did not jell. Somebody in the higher echelons had looked over the record of his last mission and judged he needed a rest. "What shall we do with Chevron, then? Post him to a satellite. Even a genius at it can't louse anything up in a satellite."

Facing the door, he was checked again by his own reflection on the inside of his plexiglass facepiece: high forehead, short-cropped brown hair, gray-flecked eyes, unsmiling—a hard, sardonic face when you got right down to it.

He bared his teeth at it, as one somber dog to another, and ducked his head to take his two meters under the lintel.

Outside, he was on an open gallery in the dormitory quadrant of the wheel. Other hatches were flipping open and a chorus line of bulky figures was stepping out for the soft-shoe shuffle to the nearest gravity trunk. Then one after another they were clawing along its steel-net sides, like so many grotesque spiders.

Three watches of twenty apiece kept N5 in continuous service. Visiting specialists of one kind and another knocked the complement to sixty-eight. For Chevron's money, there could have been a couple of hundred wedged in the operations globe when the station director plugged himself in on the general net and made an all-hands call.

When it filtered through the channels, it was a request for a head count and there was an edge on some voices as they checked in. If the old bastard only wanted to know they were there, he could have chosen a better time. There was, anyway, no place else to go.

Chevron let the rattle of responses flow on over his head. He had wedged himself between two circular ports on the raised gallery that ran around the full circumference of the globe and could look down on the action on the operations floor.

A large scanner was monitoring the launch of a squat recovery module. As it came out of the trap glowing bright orange, there was a gap in the report sequence and he filled it with his own reference.

"Four-five-one oblique seven zero oblique Charlie nine Chevron."

Although it was his own, it sounded strange to his ear. He recognized that he had not used it much over the last few years. There was a point there: enough to send a man schizo in time.

There was a digestive pause as the last resident filed his serial. The director, Dr. Vernon Greer, raised a gauntlet to tug at his right earlobe, as he did under stress, found himself thwarted by the smooth carapace of his visor and went on to tear a strip from the output of his console and read it off in his high-pitched quaver: "Two-six-four oblique seven-five monkey five zero. Martinez."

As a payoff for the exercise it was a dead flop. Chevron, with a trained memory for names and faces, saw Lois Martinez as a full-color inset on the scanner. She was a small neat brunette, Semitic, a natural for an Assyrian frieze. She worked in the station medicare unit. Her supple fingers, as he recalled, had run appreciatively over his bicep when she took a sample for the routine blood count.

He was therefore ready to be surprised when Greer cleared his throat with a crackle that echoed in every dome and said, "I have to tell you that Miss Martinez opened the lock in the shuttle launch bay and went out of the station. She was not wearing a suit. Death would be instantaneous. I have taken the unusual step of assem-

bling all personnel to underline the gravity . . . er . . .
seriousness of the situation. I need not remind you that
this is the second case in the month. It has not happened
before in my experience. Therefore we must be on constant guard. Until further notice no one should be alone
at any time. Suitable pairing will be worked out for both
on and off-duty periods. This will mean longer on-watch
duties until investigations have been made. But we cannot take the risk of this happening again. Dr. Kuhlmann
will work out details. Do not leave until your partner has
been nominated. Are there any questions?"

Chevron looked at his time disk. As far as time had
any relevance on the station, it was 0200 on the nose,
seven minutes since the alarm had gone. The mortal remains of Lois Martinez, liquids boiled off in the great
vacuum, would have been scooped into a disposal sack.
Greer had acted promptly and come up with the only
reasonable plan. But it was going to make things difficult.
A constant shadow checking his every move would end
any usefulness he might have. Could Greer have thought
that one out? Or had somebody else put the idea into his
head?

On balance, it was likely that he was simply going by
the book. Space played tricks with personnel; even the
homely run within Earth's gravisphere had been known
to work an insidious flanker on the human spirit. There
was the case in the archives of the old Goodyear project,
one of the first weather satellites with a crew of forty,
hand-picked staff. It had been found empty, an electronic *Marie Celeste,* and no investigation had ever come
up with a reason.

The crowd was thinning out. Only the watch on deck
supplemented by some extra hands still remained at the
coal face when Chevron's number came out of the bag.

He was paired with eight-eight-four oblique six zero oblique Baker four two four, Beukes.

They shuffled off together. Jack Beukes, a small tubby man carrying a torch for humor in the teeth of adversity, put on a high falsetto and said, "Shall we go to your room or mine, dear? Ha Ha." He ended most transmissions with a double bark that could pass for an encouraging laugh to cue in the next speaker on the right note.

Chevron reckoned that life's lottery had dealt him another shrewd knock. To be closeted with Beukes for the foreseeable future would flood his gut with green bile. But he heard his own voice, a ready dissembler, answer in the same vein. "Wherever you like so long as we're together."

Chevron maneuvered successfully for his own pad and helped Beukes to shift his gear.

Beukes said, "You know something? This has me worried. I do the rounds of these cans, auditing, checking supply requisitions. And as to that, some of these directors'd put in for a herd of elephants if they weren't watched. Do you know that? On N35 last month I found a chit for a pool table, hooded lamps and all. Signed by the director in his own hand. Think of the cost of sending that up. Of course he denied it, reckoned some kook had slipped it in for a laugh. Ha ha."

Chevron sitting on his cot with depression settling like a gray cloud said, "You were saying it had you worried. Why is that—beyond the obvious bit that a good bookkeeper doesn't want to lose a lush little asset like the Martinez?"

"Oh yes. I was saying. I must be the jinx of the century. I've been around for no less than three fatalities over the last six months. This makes number four. Not like this one. Accidents. But it makes you think."

9

"On satellites?"

"Surely on satellites. N35 for one. Youngster got himself crisped in the shuttle launch bay. Ha ha."

"How did he get in there? There's an automatic seal on during launch."

"So there is. It was all investigated. Genuine five-star mechanical failure."

"And the others?"

"The same. Not the same accident of course. One lost by malfunction of an inspection vehicle. Then a girl on N30. That's a parking orbit job over the Sahara. Watches the camels and the Sphinx's inscrutable smile or some such. I never could see the use of that one. Nothing on the scanner day in and day out but undulating dunes. Will the Fuzzy Wuzzy attack the fort tonight? Pick up your musket, Ponsonby, and stand by your post like a man. Save the last round for yourself. Ha ha."

Chevron said patiently, "And what happened to that one, the girl on N30?"

"Oh. Heart. Heart packed in. Overstimulation of the vagus nerve. So you can let your imagination play with that one. Ha ha."

"Homicide then?"

"No, there was nobody charged. She'd been watching some audience participation stuff on her actualizer. A good spectator also creates. Ha ha."

Chevron reckoned enough was enough. He rummaged in the locker over his trundle bed and brought out a zip case. "I'll take a shower. Don't worry about me, Jack, I'll be all right. There's no way out except through the plug."

Beukes's voice went on muted by the sluice. Chevron, head and shoulders leaning out of the flow, made a rapid and practiced rearrangement of the components in his razor pack and plugged a small earpiece into his left ear.

A cool female voice giving nothing away said, "Go ahead." With the miniature mike pressed to his throat, Chevron said quietly, "Local problem. Regular branch should investigate. My usefulness over. Suggest transfer."

"Understood. Out."

Beukes's percussive laugh made a period. Chevron, toweling his head, rejoined the dialogue.

"What was that, Jack?"

"I said Kuhlmann has no imagination. He could have worked some pairing angles that would have been a pleasure all round. No offense meant for present company, but there's a little redhead in the Met. section that would stand a close audit. Ha ha. Mind you it could be worse. There's that big Swede, Olsen in Communications. Never says a word. I couldn't stand him. Now you I find *sympatico.*"

Breakfast in N5 was never a gourmet's rave. Chevron, shoving some nutritious pink pablum round his dish with a plastic spoon felt that he had hit rock bottom. Jack Beukes was filling his left ear with a blow-by-blow account of a station director who had duplicated replacements until he could build himself a private shuttle. Only the Beukes's eagle eye had stood between the Northern Hemisphere economy and a cool million dollar grab. "What I save them in a year, you wouldn't believe. But what do they pay me? Last quarter I was waiting six days in Freetown in the rainy season. Just sitting on my tail watching the rain go drip drip off the porch and they listed it as a leave period so I couldn't claim expenses. It makes you think. Nobody values a conscientious public servant."

Chevron said absently, "That's right, Jack. As always you have touched the living heart of the matter with a needle."

A speaker in the wardroom ceiling said, "Mr. Chevron. Please report to Dr. Kuhlmann's office."

Somebody had moved it along real fast. It was just as well. Another twelve hours and he reckoned the service would have been one auditor under strength.

Kuhlmann, a tall thin-faced man with a beaked nose and a conviction that an admin man should speak in a brisk, clipped staccato said, "Ah, Mr. Chevron. Bad business last night. Bad business. No good for morale. Morale's important on a station like this. I like to think it's a happy ship. Did you know the girl? But that's hardly likely, you've not been with us long. I've had no time to talk to you. It seems you're required elsewhere. Urgent memo came in half an hour back. Close schedule, but I think you'll make it. Vectors will be right in fifty-three minutes precisely. You're to go down to Accra where instructions will be waiting. Not very convenient from our point of view, but whoever considered that?"

Chevron said, "It's news to me. Do you have any idea where I have to go?"

"Not a word. Just the movement order, but its from the department of environmental control. Our masters, Mr. Chevron. Some desk-bound genius has a rush of blood to the head and we jump to attention."

Coming after the close session with Beukes, Chevron thought it was a little hard. Everybody was set to count him as a perambulating ear. But he held fast to the time bit. Fifty-three minutes was only a drop in the ocean of a life span.

He said, "I made some preliminary notes on the reactors. I would say that there's no major refit needed for

12

another term. But no doubt another engineer will be out to confirm that. I'll leave my incomplete report with you and you can pass it on."

At the hatch he said, "One thing. This'll leave Beukes without a watchdog. I know you like to make the best arrangements you can. He gets on well with Olsen. Preserve that happy ship bit."

"Surely. Good suggestion. I'll have to make a few changes. The director would like a word with you before you go. Good-bye, Mr. Chevron."

Off the hook, invigilation-wise Chevron took a sudden decision. He walked on past the trunk to the dormitory quadrant and took the next exit from the hub to the medicenter. Without a suit, he was along the ratlines like an apprentice with a hard casemate at his back, so fast that he had no clear idea of what he intended to do when he stood outside a double-leaf door marked with a red cross and pictograph of a white-gowned smiler holding a syringe.

Inside it was as he remembered it: a small reception area, a hard-faced blonde girl in a stiff white cap with a lapel pin saying *Iris Beavers,* and beyond her desk three hatches labeled *Station Medical Officer, Lab, Sick Bay.*

Chevron leaned both hands flat on the counter and said, "So this is where the victim worked. What had you been doing to her, then? Putting plastic mice in her tights?"

"I don't know who you are, but that's not nice. She was very happy. We can't understand it. What is it you want?"

It was a good question. Chevron thought about it. "I've been called back to base. Since I was going down today, I thought there might be something I could do. Personal effects for instance. If you could seal them up in a bag,

I'd see they were forwarded. Save a long drag through normal channels."

"Oh well. I'll see Dr. Groves. If he says it's all right."

She crossed the floor with a reserved wiggle and tapped twice below the S.M.O. legend.

A rich baritone called, "Come in, Miss Beavers," and she did, pausing only to shoot a level, reproachful look at the client.

Chevron sat on the desktop. There would have been time to take a look through the unit, but he guessed there would be no percentage in it. Station security would check around. There would be nothing lying on the floor tagged clue one.

He reached over and flipped through an appointments file. His own name was there. Personnel were listed on a ten-day cycle. Lois Martinez had gone through a routine inspection two days back. But then so had the Beavers. Both were asterisked for renewal shots of vaccine. It would be necessary to keep the medical staff at protection-plus in case they had to handle an epidemic. Nothing there. The receptionist gave no sign of being under any kind of stress.

Voices behind the door stopped. Iris Beavers reappeared followed by the top hand in person.

Groves, small to be the vehicle for the plummy voice said, "This is irregular Mr. —"

"Chevron."

"—Mr. Chevron. Highly irregular. But thoughtful of you to suggest it. A terrible affair this. Very unsettling for the staff. We have a special responsibility on a station like this. If the medical team are maladjusted, how will the rest fare? Who is to guard the guardians, eh?"

He lifted a hand as though to tap Iris Beavers where nature had made generous provision, thought better of

14

it and ran his fingers through his thinning hair. "Well, I can see no objection. The security sergeant looked through Miss Martinez's things and cleared them for return. Took copies for his file. There's an address in Dover U.K. They would certainly go quicker from a spaceport. Yes. I can agree to that. Miss Beavers will take you along to get them. She shared the room. Sign a receipt, of course."

On the way, Chevron said, "So you knew her very well. Did you see any signs of what she might do?"

"No. Nothing. Like I said. She was very happy. And if you don't mind, I'd rather not talk about it."

"Well you must see that anybody would be curious. If it's as you say, it could happen to any one of us. You for instance. Brains all over that funny hat. Perhaps she was in a jam about money. Or a man. Despairing love. Or too successful love."

Iris Beavers stopped dead and said earnestly, "Look. I told you I don't want to talk about it. She was a nice girl and a good friend. Don't go raising rumors that don't have any basis. I'll tell you this and then for the land's sake leave it. She was okay for money and generous with it. Her father gave her an allowance over and above the pay she gets here. There was no man involved or woman either, since you seem to have a twisty way of looking at anything. She was just fine. I didn't see her yesterday, because we were on awkward duties. I know her better than anybody and as far as I know, it's got no sense at all. Okay?"

It had the ring of truth. There was also genuine feeling behind it. In spite of appearances, Iris Beavers felt it as a personal loss.

Cheveron said gently, "That's all right, Iris. I'm sorry. But questions are bound to be asked. I guess it's nothing to do with me, anyway. Would you like to write a note to her father? I'll see it gets to him."

To his surprise, the girl's eyes suddenly filled with tears and she turned away, angry to be caught out.

"I'll do that, if there's time. All this makes me mad. It's so unfair. She just didn't deserve to go like that. It just doesn't make any sense."

Standing in the launch bay waiting for a maintenance crew to finish tanking up the shuttle, Chevron wrapped it up in his mind and labeled it with the same tag. It didn't make any sense. But it was a domestic matter. Satellite security branch would sieve it fine and make a report. It had no bearing on the international scene. Or was he really past it, as his last confidential profile hinted, punch drunk with too much action and too little time to stand and stare?

Beukes's voice cut into the reverie. It was on the breathy side as though he had pushed his motor against the clock to make the tryst. "Ah, Mark. Glad I just caught you. You didn't say anything about moving on. Unfinished business? It's a pity when we were getting on so well. Damon and Pythias, ha ha. I know you won't mind if I ask you to do something for me. Just a letter to my sister. Write to her every week. She's all the family left and she likes me to keep in touch. It'll go faster from a trading post. Bring a little cheer into a drab life, ha ha."

"Surely."

Chevron shoved the packet into an outside pouch. The pilot was in. He saved himself any more earache by flipping forward his casque and was *incommunicado*. He waved a gauntlet in general blessing and followed the pilot through the hatch.

Taking nearly 5g's as the shuttle made a corrective course change, Chevron felt the line of the fresh scar that

16

crossed from his right shoulder to his left hip as though it had been drawn again with a hot knife. Maybe the department had a case. It had been a failure in concentration that had allowed the opposition to get so close. He had been sidetracked by a personal involvement that he should not have had.

On the threshold of blackout, he could see the tableau as it had been, with the Iranian girl Paula kneeling by his open case rifling through the lining with a practiced hand —the same hand that had moved expertly through his hair as though it wanted to make a long term occupation of it.

Everything had become clear. All the bits had fallen into place. He, Mark Chevron, one of the half-dozen top operators in the department, had been taken for a ride by a smooth brown *houri* hardly out of high school.

Even then with her eyes giving it all away, he had been slow. Oval face serious and purely businesslike, she had judged the angles and come to her decision while he was still coping with his sense of loss and waste. A small neat blaster had appeared in her hand and she was shooting a thin searing line across the room before he had sorted himself out.

Only Blackett following up and unseen by her had saved his life.

To Blackett, she was a rag, a rope and a hank of hair and hostile at that. He had bisected her forehead with a single clinical shot.

Pressure eased and the vision receded into the holographic web of memory, leaving only a sense of long smooth sides and round high breasts under his hand. God, he must have been simpleminded. It would not happen again. But then it should not have happened at all.

The pilot was saying, "All right, Mr. Chevron? Sorry

about that. Those zombies on N5 had it a fraction wrong. I had to make a bigger correction. They'd have had us down in Brazzaville."

Chevron said thickly, "Fine. I'm okay."

That would have been a nasty twist for the department. Set up on an interrogation machine, he would have been a scoop for Southern Hem Intelligence. Not that he could have allowed it to happen. Articles were clear enough. He would have been duty-bound to bite into the oblivion capsule in the strap of his time disk.

How would he feel about that? It was late in the day to have second thoughts. He shoved it away to the back of his mind with other unresolved jetsam and watched the white city of Accra grow as if in a zoom lens.

At street level, the image of a soaring marble city took a knock. It was mostly stucco and gimcrack at that. There was the pervasive half-rotten, half-spicy smell that he remembered and heat that fell like a tangible weight that could not be shrugged off.

He checked in at The Midnight Sun where two-thirds of the lobby roof was taken up by a bulging blood-red hemisphere and a black clerk in a red tarboosh had to shift a chameleon to work on his register.

Following a company rule, Chevron checked through his room. If it was wired for sound or vision it was not obvious. But a miniaturized pickup could be sharing a hole wiith a woodworm. He could only be ninety percent sure it was clean.

He took the sealed bag of Lois Martinez's effects and a fine watchmaker's toolkit and sat on his bed with his feet straight out in front of him. Ten minutes patient work had the Environment Control Department crest neatly sheared away in one piece and the flap opened.

He tipped the contents out beside him and returned the items one by one. There was an octagonal time disk on an electrum bracelet; a ring with a chunky amethyst in an oblong bezel; a springy gold spiral with a strand of fine black hair wound in it, as though it had been pulled free in a hurry; a wide belt of oblong bronze plates with a serpent clasp; a bronze Celtic type armlet; a covering letter no doubt from Greer; and a diary bound in red Moroccan leather.

He flipped through the pages. She had recorded something every day: nothing of earth-shattering importance, but small things she had noticed about people. She even had a five-point scale to rate them on. Beukes's arrival got a mention. He gave her the green creeps. Listed with an E underscored twice. She was affectionate, shrewd, interested in people. If it was anything at all it was not the diary of a potential suicide.

Chevron saw his own name, rated A with a query. Also his scar got an honorable mention. "Supposed to be an industrial accident. But I don't believe it. More like a burn from a high-frequency beam. Tissue damage would go with that. When I touched his arm, he gave me a very considering look. Hard to get to know really well, I should think. A solitary man. Stands back. But if he did let himself go, he'd be terrific."

The last day had no entry. Maybe she did her writing in the evening and events had overtaken her. The last entry confirmed it timewise.

"Very depressed all day. Never felt like this before. What's the point of being here? What's the point of eating and working and sleeping and doing it over again the next day? I don't think I could stand another day like today."

There it was. He could visualize her wearing the gear, pretty and full of sap and *brio*. Now she was dead and it stank. It was senseless, a random cruelty.

He shoved the things back in the bag and resealed it. Then he weighed Beukes's letter in his hand. There seemed no point in doing anything about that; but he could at least be thorough.

It could have been Beukes speaking: rambling sentences and so many qualifying sidetracks that it was almost impossible to make any sense out of it. He put it out flat on his dressing chest and stood a reading lamp beside it. Then he rummaged in his kit for the collection of items that plugged together to make a miniature camera, slipped a reel of microfilm from the filter of a cigarette and took pictures of each sheet. Somebody else could have a look at that. It would at least show that he was working at his craft.

Sixteen hundred hours on the clock. Coming up to sundowner time. Chevron mailed the packages, including a small one of his own, and hired a sand car to take him out to the beach.

It was open, without sides, a small mobile tray with exaggerated hoops fore and aft, so that the eager young could ride standing, with their hair flying back gallantly.

Some of the heat was going out of the day. There was a lot of traffic on the beach road. At this time the town emptied in a stampede for the sea.

Three kilometers on, he drove through a rainbow arch cleverly cantilevered on one slender foot. Labadi Beach was picked out in colored lights already switched on so as not to be surprised by the short equatorial twilight.

Chevron left the trolley in a parking lot that was filling up as though through a sluice and picked his way through the crowd to the long esplanade that lined the bay.

Color was brilliant, a shifting pattern of gold ocher, viridian, cobalt, alizarine, all set off by skins of ivory black or dark brown. All the women seemed to walk well, with a pleasing wiggle that rattled costume jewelry and sent out vibrations as of a vast harem.

There were some paler skins about, enough to make him unremarkable. He took a surfboard from a stack under a palm tree and went down a ramp onto the beach itself.

At the water's edge, he followed the agreeable custom of the country, dumped his bush shirt and shorts and went on into the sea carrying his board, the original forked animal stripped of artifice.

Fifty meters out in warm racing water, he edged into a long comber, judged its fall and flung himself forward.

It was a suspended moment in time: speed, noise, surf beating at his skin, complete isolation until the landfall in fine abrasive sand. A girl appeared out of the shallows at his elbow, hair sleeked into a skull cap, water streaming from carved ebony shoulders and running from the tips of her taut breasts.

The quick and the dead. He was tangibly alive and the Martinez girl was dead. Being and no being, a dichotomy with no clues offered for the connection.

After three more trips, he shifted along the beach. Time to look for his contact, Poldano. The American would be somewhere about at this time. It was hardly likely that any instructions would have come out yet. But he should register that he was there present, all ready to leap about.

For twenty minutes he drifted with each run to cover the beach. Then he began to work back. Almost at the point where he had left his shirt, there was a knot of people round a sand truck that had come out from the Coastguard station.

Ears battered by the surf, it was a half-minute before he adjusted to the novel sound. A good hectore of Labadi beach had gone quiet like a stretch of jungle reacting to a threat.

With his board under his arm, he nudged into the rear rank. Two beach guards had nipped smartly from the back of the truck with a stretcher and went out of sight to sand level.

When they reappeared, less spry under the load, they had a long pale-brown body on the canvas. As they lifted it aboard, he had a full-face view.

It was Chad Poldano, mute, bearded, with a run of blood from the corner of his mouth and a fish-stalker's harpoon sticking out of his chest like a marker.

II

CHEVRON PULLED into a lay-by, a palm grove fitted out with rustic tables and backless settles. He was ahead of the return rush. After a digestive pause the *hoi polloi* had gone back to filling every minute with a distance run.

He left the trolley and walked slowly into the bush as if one of nature's recurrent errands. Not that there were any visible watchers to register the fact. But he reckoned that no one would plant a bug on every tree.

Leaning with his back to a smooth bole where he could see the road, he took out his communicator. He would have liked to answer the cool "Go ahead" with Poldano's dictum, "Never linger under a palm tree. You never know when a coconut will fall." It would have been a suitably quirky obituary; but he reckoned it would not be appreciated.

Instead he said, "Poldano is dead. Instructions."

"Wait."

Two cars went past in a wow of speed. Behind the continual muted chatter of bush noise, he could hear a drum, very soft and insistent. That would go on all night. There were still primitive communities even near the modern city that refused to be absorbed in the twenty-fourth century of progress.

Maybe they had a point at that. Lois Martinez would have been no worse off pounding grain in a quern to a ripe age. Environmental control only made it possible for more human beings to live, under stress. The good life was as illusionary as it had ever been. Man lechered after the unattainable. But then again if he stopped doing that he would be nothing at all.

It was a dubious mental trail and the voice speaking out of the palm of his hand sidetracked him from it.

"You are to *stay* there. Do nothing about Poldano. Take a *vacation*. Call in every second day. Out."

Chevron snapped the case shut and considered its lid with the blue and gold semicircle of laurel leaves. That was Wagener's fine Italian hand. It was Wagener who had wanted to ground him for a six month's suspension. He had said, "I know your record, Chevron. But the past is no basis. Believe me, your own interest is involved. Nobody stays in the top slot forever. We can't afford a weak link. It isn't fair to others who would depend on you. You see that?"

True, all true. He would have been the first to complain if an unreliable operator had been foisted on himself. But a man should be allowed one error of judgement.

God, what did they think he would do? Stand in the market and shout that he was Poldano's friend?

There was a thud at his feet. A massive yellow-green pod was embedded in the loam. Maybe they had a point. He couldn't even take good advice. If he had been standing twenty centimeters farther out he would have been driven in like any picket.

It was as if Poldano's *ka* had dropped it as a last gesture before following the sun boat over the rim of the bay. Chevron lit a cigarette in broad daylight and sat in his trolley, giving lateral thinking a chance.

When he finished it, he was isolated in black night and the butt made a glowing tracer as he flicked it into the bush.

He had ranged round the topic without making a head-on attempt at solving it. There was always pressure from Southern Hem intelligence. Not always at the same level and not always at the same point. But they jockeyed

24

round for the advantage and if they had a scheme on, they were prepared to go real slow and set everything up to the last detail.

As far as the department knew, there was nothing big on the way. That was why he had been drafted to N5 to check its security readiness: a non-job to keep his mind off sin, covered by some interesting work in his civilian line as a thermonuclear engineer. But they could be wrong. Knocking off Poldano could be a starting move in some devious ploy—a feint in fact to draw attention from a real move elsewhere.

But where, for God's sake? The uneasy peace between the two hemispheres was as secure as it had ever been over the last decade. There was even a standing conference on a total amalgamation which would unify the planet for the first time in its history.

Now that would really be something—if it was what they really wanted. But maybe nobody would accept that last step and banish aggression altogether. It was too important a building brick in the human psyche. No dialectic, no struggle, even if it was an artificial one, and the race would fall apart from the center.

Where then? Farthest, geographically, was the North Pole. What would the satraps of Brazilia want with the North Pole? Nothing that they couldn't do with their own Antarctica.

Lateral thinking had not taken him far. He started the motor and edged out into the highway. Decision came with movement. Wagener could get himself knotted. He would take a look for himself at Poldano's place.

Chevron turned off the bush road where a slab crossed the open drain ditch and threshed on into undergrowth until he was hidden.

25

Not that he had seen any fellow travelers. Fifteen kilometers out of Accra on the Kumasi road, he had forked right onto a beaten earth track, heavily corrugated and running in a continuous tunnel of overhanging trees.

Poldano's bungalow was on rising ground about two kilometers from the junction and half a kilometer farther on, the first house of a small community compound which housed some of the European staff of a tropical medicine research center. There was a clearing with a pool and a small helicopter pad.

Chevron walked on the paved edge of the ditch. Without the hum of the motor and the thrash of treads on the ridgetops, he could get the night noises strength nine.

There was a drum fairly near and another one on a different rhythm a long way off. It made the idea of long-distance communication entirely credible. For that matter it would straddle the equatorial line. Southern Hem had a big garrison in Gabon and every kind of early warning device. They could be using it as an open link, so commonplace that nobody ever noticed it.

Maybe now, very now, a coal-black drummer glistening with sweat in a banana grove was putting out a stop press that he had left Accra and was making for Poldano's compound.

Out of the moving airstream it was still hot enough and his shirt was clinging to his chest. He took it off and carried it hooked by the tab over one shoulder. A car came from ahead moving fast, lights filling the tunnel. He dropped into the ditch and stayed on hands and knees in a two-centimeter deep cushion of white dust.

Five minutes later the road began to rise and turned to climb the spur on which the compound stood.

As he remembered it, there was a gatehouse with a barrier and a duty porter to record visitors. He followed the road round the bluff until it was doubling back on itself and the compound was a nimbus of light on the crown of the hill. On his right hand there was solid rock with the occasional palm tree growing straight out of a crevice and turning up with a smooth elbow.

He got his hands on the nearest and hauled himself up. Security-wise it made a nonsense of the checkpoint, except that it would put a physical limit on the gear that could be lifted out by this route.

At the top, there was a corroded fence jutting out at an angle to make an overhang. He followed it along to a secure picket, pitched his shirt over the top, then went out hand-over-hand until he was hanging free, hauled himself up in the sweat of his brow and went down the inside like a crab.

There was a broad belt of shrubbery on the perimeter and beyond it bright daylight from four batteries of floods on gantries at each corner.

The pool was in use. He could hear voices and the splash of water. Keeping behind the bush screen he edged round to the gatehouse. The barrier was down and the porter had gone inside his round adobe hut.

Poldano's bungalow had a verandah with three broad steps. It was roofed with yellow shingles, double-fronted with a swing screen of white gauze, surrounded by plain grass lawns and separated from the next in line by about fifty meters. Somebody was home. The right-hand front room was lit from inside and there was a glow in depth beyond the screen door.

Chevron crossed twenty meters of open ground moving lightly as a cat, veered left and passed a gable end with a long window which would have a view over the cliff in daylight.

Round the back, there was the same neat lawn stretching away to the shrubbery. Poldano had it set up so that nobody could get too near without breaking cover.

There was singing in the kitchen, a lugubrious chant with the rhythm taken up now and again by a succession of knocks as though with a spoon on a hollow panel. Chevron edged along a meter-wide concrete footing and looked in the galley.

A thickset African with a shaven head and a white housecoat was sitting on a high stool holding a solitary wake, turned in on himself in a private dialogue.

It was Zakayo. He had been with Poldano for the last ten years. There was no doubt he had been told the score.

Chevron eased down the door release and was inside before the man could move.

He said, "Easy now. Easy, Zakayo. You remember me. I visited Dr. Poldano about two years ago."

Zakayo was drumming with a knife haft and spun round with his arm back ready to throw.

Chevron felt his scar tingle along its length. He said again, "Easy. Think about it." At the same time he was ready to swing his shirt into the path the knife would take, with one part of his mind ice cold and working on reaction times, the likely trajectory and the speed of flight.

Zakayo's face suddenly split into a wide grin showing a massive set of white choppers and a very red tongue. It was a rictus that did not spread to the eyes, but a valid bit of the gestural dance of welcome. He also said, "Surely I remember you, Mr. Chevron. I guess I was a little hasty. Come right in. I'll make some coffee. I was just thinking what I ought to do. For one sure thing I'd like to twist the head off of the bastard who fired that fish spear into my boss."

"How did you know I would know about that?"

"Come now, Mr. Chevron. I know the doctor was go-

28

ing to meet somebody. Then one hour ago I get this news from the medicenter. Then you come in looking for something, not calling at the front porch like a regular visitor. It's pretty plain, Mr. Chevron. There's a connection. I never thought Mr. Chad would go like that. He's been pretty close before, but he's always got clear. He was a good man. Very smart. It would take somebody very good to fix him this way."

"Any ideas?"

"No, Mr. Chevron. Like I said, he had to meet somebody on the beach."

"That was me. But we never made contact. Was there any fall-back message?"

"Nothing. Nothing I know of. But take a look, Mr. Chevron. Accra security were here. They found nothing. They said for me to stay on here until I hear anything different."

"That's right. He'd like to think you were looking after things. But take care. Whoever did it will have this address. They might want to find out what you know."

"That's not much, Mr. Chevron. The doctor was pretty close. But I've been with him a long time and I know he was something else beside what he did in this unit. I think a lot in here, but I say nothing."

Zakayo tapped his forehead with the haft of his kitchen knife, climbed down from his stool and prepared to do the honors of the house.

At ground level, he was shorter than at first appeared. Shoulders and chest were massive and would have suited a frame taller than Chevron's two meters. But the legs were stocky and he had to look up to meet Chevron's eye. He kept his knife and slipped it in a narrow pocket up the sleeve of his housecoat.

Very nimble in spite of his bulk, he led into the living

room where the light was and made for a drinks trolley behind a bamboo screen.

"You'd like a drink, Mr. Chevron? The doctor always had whisky and lime at this time."

"That suits me. Have something yourself."

"The doctor was a good man, Mr. Chevron. Always the same. Not one of those who change from day to day and you never know where you are. There aren't many like him. Always pleasant and easy to get on with. I'll miss him, I don't mind telling you. It won't be the same."

"What will you do?"

"That I don't know. I expect there'll be another man brought in to take his place in the medical unit and this house goes with the job. But I don't know whether to stay on. I've got a cousin in Accra. Runs a private car hire business. I have an interest in that. Sleeping partner, you might say. I could take up my option. But it wouldn't be the same. I liked working with the Doctor. He used to sit in that chair and we'd argue the toss. All sorts of things. Only last night, he was on about another ice age. Did you know that both Northern and Southern Hem have a whole department working on that? If it wasn't for the polar stations it could begin any time."

"I've heard about it. What set him off on that tack?"

"He'd been reading an old copy of a New Zealand Scientific Review. The loose pages in the rack there somewhere. Ice builds up in the southern cap. When it gets so thick the weight makes it melt at the bottom. Then there's a surge of ice out over the sea. Right down as far as fifty degrees south. This reflects sunlight back and the Earth gets colder."

Chevron freshened his drink and walked over to the window picking out the flimsy single sheet of newsprint on the way. It could only be a coincidence. On the other hand Poldano was shrewd. Some hint of action in the north could have triggered his interest.

"You remembered it well."

"The doctor made it very clear. I reckon you could learn about anything the way he explained it. With the Earth cooling the northern cap would grow. More heat would be reflected into space and glaciers would push down all over Europe. Also sea level would rise maybe twenty or thirty meters. He reckoned we'd be all right on this bluff. But it would cause a whole lot of grief."

"Which is why the polar stations keep at it. It's an interesting theory, but it won't happen."

"Just what I said, Mr. Chevron. It's in nobody's interest. Now if Southern Hem could fix it so that it only happened in the north, I guess there'd be something to worry over. But they'd not cut off their own nose to spite their face."

Chevron folded the paper small and shoved it in the breast pocket of his bush jacket. "Have you any objection if I take a look round? He was expecting to see me. It's just possible there's a message or something he wanted me to have."

"Help yourself, Mr. Chevron. Would you like for me to fix a meal?"

"That would have been okay. But I shouldn't stay that long. I came in over the fence and I'll go out that way. If you're asked you haven't seen me."

"I understand, Mr. Chevron. You can trust me."

Poldano's room was clinically neat. Chevron stood just inside the door without putting on a room light, letting his eyes get used to the little light he had, and let his mind sift the data: single bed with a green cover; woven straw mat; dressing chest with a delicately carved okapi about ten centimeters tall set in the middle with mathematical accuracy; white closet with stainless steel ring handles and louvred front; ground glass door to a bathroom; half-glassed door leading out to the gable end and an extension of the front verandah.

Seeing it in fact rather than in imagination, he recognized that there was no point in a search. Poldano was too old a hand to leave anything about. Instructions would be in his head. Reports would be passed on. Any ideas he had could only be reached now by a good medium. He put on his shirt and stopped with the second button fastened.

A slight scuff from the verandah had him moving across and flattening himself on the hinge side of the door.

The lever moved down and the door began to open.

Somebody else was interested. Southern Hem for a gold clock. It was only surprising they had left it so long. That was good. Balance the account and maybe get a little information at the same time.

The door came back half a meter and began to close. His mind was sending out a tickertape. *One only and a thin one at that.* At the same time he went into action, shoving his right knee into the panel to slam it shut and continuing the turn so that he rammed the new arrival flat against the closing door. Any backup operator outside shooting through the glass would hit his own man first.

Data acquisition network went into overload. Fine silky hair was brushing his chin. Skin was marble smooth. Elasticity factors were all wrong for a male subject. There was a scent compounded of sandalwood. The startled "oh" choked off by his hand was in the alto register. He had gotten himself a female and a taut and nubile one at that.

Still holding her mouth shut, he continued his turn in

a follow-through that rolled her away from the door and waited for a count of five.

After a brief struggle which must have told her that resistance was futile she had gone still. Eyes in the semi-gloom, very bright and almost all pupil, glared at him over his hand.

There was no sound from outside. Chevron said, "Who are you? Say it quietly and know for a truth that I'd just as soon break your neck as not." At the same time, he intelligently moved his hand from her mouth and transferred it to her throat.

Surprised she might be, but she was nobody's hey-you. "I could ask you the same. Where is Dr. Poldano?"

It was a genuine query, carrying conviction. She really did not know. But then he had been convinced before. Only a fool made the same mistake twice. Chevron's fingers tightened on the smooth column.

He said harshly, "I'll ask the questions. Who are you?"

Sudden pain made tears stand out in her eyes.

"I am Dr. Riley."

"That tells me everything. Be more specific."

"Four-nine-three oblique seven five oblique Roger nine one, Riley Doctor."

"Don't play about, Riley."

Pressure increased by a fraction and she added hastily, "I work here. With Dr. Poldano. I've just come off duty and I was looking for him."

"Why not use the front door like a regular visitor?"

"We are friends. I always use this door."

"Loving friends?"

There was silence. Only the eyes told him that she hated his guts—also that he had touched the living heart of the matter with a needle. A blunt one.

33

But it cleared up one point. She did not know he was dead.

Hearing voices Zakayo padded in at his back. The handy kitchen knife appeared over Chevron's shoulder. "Let me work him over, boss." Then a change of tone. "Miss Ann. It's all right, Mr. Chevron. She's not one of them. She wouldn't have hurt the doctor. She's okay. It's Dr. Riley. From the unit. A mind-bender."

Chevron let his hands fall to his sides. The majority vote had it.

Hands massaging her neck, she said huskily, "Will you tell me what's going on? What did you mean, Zakayo? Has Dr. Poldano been hurt?"

Chevron said brutally, "He's dead."

It was as though he had to wound somebody, to lance his own blister of black bile. But as a personal therapy it had no success. Half his mind said, *Chevron, you are the louse of all time.*

The opinion was shared by the girl. In some ways it broke the impact of the message. Pride and professional curiosity needled her to an attack.

"What satisfaction can you get in telling me like that? Did you expect me to scream or faint off?"

"This is no game. I wanted to know if you already knew."

"In spite of what I said? Don't you believe anything you hear? And what's the conclusion if I might ask? Do I pass your crude test?"

She brushed past him, walked over to the bed as if she was going to sit on it, thought better of it and veered off towards the dressing chest.

Chevron said, "That's four questions. I'm ninety-nine percent convinced, but it's the one percent that causes trouble in this business."

She had come to anchor opposite the chest with her palms flat against its top drawer and her head bent. Wings of raven-black hair swung forward, hiding her face except for the smooth line of the jaw. Her voice was firm enough, but the control was a deliberate exercise of will.

"I'd like to take this okapi. We bought it together on a trip up country. I have one like it. They make a pair."

"Do that. You could also arrange for the rest of his personal things to be sent on. Would you know what to do?"

"There is nobody. He had no family."

Chevron let the simple statement echo round his head. It was a suitable epitaph for any one of them in the department. No hostages to fortune. Expendable. On the other hand it made then vulnerable. Everybody had a yen to be important to some person somewhere. Poldano had a good thing going with this Riley girl. He himself had been a pushover for Paula.

Poldano seemed to have done better. All very neat and cosy. The best of both worlds. If you could say that of a man impaled on a fish spear.

Chevron said, "He was on the beach today. Do you know who he would be likely to be with? Why didn't you go along for instance?"

Ann Riley turned from the chest holding the okapi in both hands. Two tears rolled down her cheeks, keeping pace, adding to her air of symmetry and good proportion. She ignored them, neither hiding them nor excusing them like a good psychologist giving grief its due season. "He belonged to the Aqualife Club in Accra. They have a place on the esplanade for members to store their gear, locker room, clubroom and restaurant. He would start out from there. We can't, couldn't often go together, because we share the work at this unit. When there's an experiment on, one of us would stay. He wasn't keen to go today; but he said something had come up and he had to be around in case he was needed."

So even Poldano had slipped out of isolation. That was more than he should have said. He must have trusted his co-worker. Wagener wouldn't have liked that at all.

Ann Riley was looking over his shoulder with a totally new expression. It was her night for method training. Even before a sibilant voice said, "Stay just as you are. Don't anybody move," Chevron knew he had allowed himself to be outflanked. Wagener had the right of it. He wasn't to be trusted with a kindergarten picnic.

There were three of them, moving silently on foam-soled sneakers. With nice economy, each had picked his own target. Fine gray mesh made a uniform blank of their faces, except that the nearer one who had lined his snub blaster on Chevron's chest appeared to have a spade beard. They were in bush shirts and khaki drill slacks. Hands were pale mahogany. They had been in the country some time.

The leading hand spoke again. "Friends of the departed holding a seance. The black one is in the right place. Dr. Riley has or had a personal angle; but what would the big ugly one want? Let's hear from you. Name for a start. Just to see if it makes any sense in my head."

Chevron reckoned that anyone with a beard and his head in a bag was pushing it to make personal jibes, but the blaster put him in a privileged group. He said frankly, "Chevron's the name. I just got in town and came to look up an old acquaintance. But it seems he had an accident. If this is a robbery you're out of luck. I keep my tiara in the vaults."

The man said, "Now isn't that nice, I've gotten me a

humorist. Step over by the girl. Take them all next door, Gomez. I'll talk to them when I'm through here."

The smallest of the trio fished in a pocket and brought out another blaster. Eyes behind the gauze were expressive enough—he would like to have an opportunity to use one or both.

Chevron said mildly, "It seems we have no choice. After you, Dr. Riley. Do as the man says."

She was watching him with something like contempt, as though she had expected a more positive lead, but she walked out behind Zakayo, moving with a neat action that was not lost on Gomez.

Behind them they heard the crash of the first drawer in the chest being tipped out on the floor, then a series of sharp cracks.

They were going to be thorough. Every item would be reduced to matchwood.

Gomez lined them up along the bamboo screen and sat across a chair with his arms comfortably chocked on the rail. He looked all set for a long wait.

Chevron said hospitably, "Can I get you a drink? There's a trolley handy. We could all use one for that matter." He took a step to his right and a shaft of brilliant light jetted from Gomez's left hand.

There was a smell of singed hair and a sharp burn along his right temple. Gomez said equably. "Don't do it, son. You make me nervous. Next time, it's right between the eyes. I wouldn't like that. My chief wants to talk to you and he'd be put out. That's not good. He can be very mean and he wouldn't understand. Just stay right up close to that cool *bint*."

Zakayo's hands had shot above his head in a clear mime of cooperation and Gomez went on, "That's the idea. That fat black one has the right of it. He might live out the night. Put your hands down, Sam."

Chevron moved again and Gomez's eyes flicked back to him. Zakayo's arms came down. There was a brief flash as the long blade of the kitchen knife caught the light, and twin arcs of flame as Gomez fired both blasters into the parquet by convulsive reflex.

Chevron was already beside the chair, easing the body down as it fell. Zakayo joined him and they spread him out.

Chevron said, "Nice timing. Can you use one of these?"

"I'll stick to my knife. Thanks all the same, boss." He pulled it free and wiped it on Gomez's bush jacket, then used the point to slit the gauze mask.

Seen clear, it was plain that Gomez had died an astonished man. Otherwise there was no gain. He was a stranger.

Ann Riley, still clutching her okapi, had not moved. Breaking noises from the bedroom triggered her off. She said unexpectedly, "I can use one. Give one to me."

Chevron pitched it across and she caught it one-handed. He said curtly, "Stay where you are. Use it if you have to," and padded out through the open door.

Poldano's boudoir was a wreck. The floor round the bed was ankle-deep in black granules from an emptied mattress. One man had begun to cut out sections of the woven matting that formed the ceiling. He was half-hidden by a hanging flap.

The spokesman of the outfit was out of sight in the bathroom.

Chevron fired a dropping burst into the mat, judging where a man's head would be relative to the legs he could see. There was a brief scream that cut off in mid-flow; noises from the washroom stopped in sympathy.

Chevron could understand the man's dilemma. He would know that his schedule was all to hell; but how to get back the initiative was another matter.

To help him to a decision Chevron said, "Throw your gun out and follow it real slow." Zakayo with his knife poised delicately by the tip had a fixed grin with no element of humor in it. He said "Cover me, Boss. I'll go and winkle the bastard out."

Chevron picked a way through the debris until he was a meter from the half-open door. Then he hurled himself through, twisting as he went so that he ended up flat against the remains of an inner wall, questing for a target.

Either by design or good luck the bearded man had gotten himself a bolt hole. Over beyond the tub a long oblong panel of the partition wall had been prised away. A prudent operator, he had cut his losses and gone for bush.

Not without company. He had made a detour through the dayroom and collected a hostage. The okapi was there with its legs in the air on a rug. But Ann Riley was gone, leaving only a faint trace of sandalwood as a proof that she had appeared briefly on the muster.

III

MARK CHEVRON leaned both hands on the verandah rail and watched a steel-gray shuttle rise vertically from the front lawn, hover at its ceiling of fifty meters and turn slowly to pick up a course. As it accelerated away towards Accra, Zakayo said, "That's no good, Boss. No good at all. Dr. Riley's a fine woman. The doctor thought a lot about her and that's a fact. What will he do with her?"

"Nothing she's going to like and that's another fact."

"Do you want that I should call the precinct security? There's a post five kilometers down the road?"

It was said with so much doubt that Chevron guessed there had been other times when Poldano himself had put in a veto on a similar offer.

"No. Security won't find her. If they knew about that one he wouldn't be around flashing his beaver. Is there a car?"

"The doctor had it down at the beach. It hasn't been brought in yet. Dr. Riley has one. Only a surface trolley. They called one from the hire company in Accra when they wanted to make a long trip."

"Go borrow that. I have one to pick up down the road. You can drive me down to it. Save a little time. I'll take a look at the Aqualife Club."

"What about Dr. Riley?"

"Not a chance. If she's any use to them they'll keep her. If not she'll be picked out of the harbor—in whatever pieces the piranha leave."

Zakayo looked hard at him as if trying to judge whether it was true or false, decided it was true and turned away without comment. He disappeared out of the light from the verandah at a shambling trot.

Left alone, Chevron walked through each room. There was no time for a close search and in any case, he reckoned would be wasted labor. He dragged Gomez into the wrecked bedroom to join his filletted friend and made a pyre of books and splintered wood.

Zakayo appeared on the porch.

"I have it, Boss. Ready to go."

"Okay. Do you have anything you want to take out of the house? It'll burn like tinder. Look as though these two got themselves trapped."

Zakayo hesitated, then: "No. I guess that's all right with me. Make a clean start, as you might say."

Chevron set his blaster for a broad-angle burst and sprayed slowly over the pile. Material browned, blackened, fell in on itself and then suddenly ignited with a crack. Vermilion flowered from the heap and climbed up the hanging ceiling mats.

They backed away from an instant inferno.

At the car, Zakayo stopped and began to run back. Chevron, expecting a fire alarm any second, called impatiently, "What is it, man? Come back."

But Zakayo was already lumbering over the smoke-filled verandah. He reappeared with the okapi under his arm and a deprecating grin. "She was very fond of this, Boss. If she's alive, I know she'd like to have it."

Chevron accelerated away in a burst of power that threw the African back into his seat.

The car was known and the check barrier was lifting before they reached it. Chevron stormed down the twisting road, wheels sliding on loose gravel within centimeters of the long drop, lights boring out over the plain or bringing the cliff face into brilliant relief.

41

When they slid to a halt with locked wheels, he sai
"This is it. Take the car on into Accra if you like. I ho
you do well with your cousin. If necessary you can sa
that Dr. Riley asked you to pick her up in Accra, but sl
didn't turn up at the RV. You were not in the house whe
the fire started."

"Two things, Boss. Nobody's going to believe tha
They'll pull the vital evidence clause and have me on
truth machine in thirty minutes flat. Secondly, I'd like
go with you. You could need somebody to watch yo
back. I know the score. I used to help the doctor."

"The devil you did. He was way out of line bringing a
other helper in."

There was only a glimmer of eyes and teeth to ma
Zakayo's position in space. But they were eloquent enoug
What the hell. He was out of line himself at this point.

Chevron came to a decision. "All right then. Follow n
in this car. Leave it in a park at the city limits."

Zakayo's Cheshire-cat grin hung in the darkness. "Yc
won't regret it, Boss. I want one chance to square wi
the creep who fixed the doctor. I'll stick right behind you

From the bluff a column of smoke and flame we
straight up like a signal fire. The nearest drumbeat brol
rhythm, changed to a carrier of single percussive knock
then went off on a new tack with a roll.

Chevron said, "Who are they telling?"

"I don't know, Boss. Just naturally talkative I gues
But for what it's worth they'll know all about it in Acc
before we get there."

Driving alone again, Chevron considered it. The trad
tional communication net could have its uses. They mig
even have a line on Ann Riley, if she was finally delivere
to some point in the interior. Not that she would repa
finding. Working on her for a quick pay-off, they wou

42

tear into her mind with direct-access gear that would leave her a zombie if she stayed alive at all.

Unconsciously he had flogged the car to its ceiling and was beating out into the feed lane of the highway with two wheels off the ground.

But Zakayo was staying close, no doubt grinning silently to his reflection in the windshield. He was a strange one.

Chevron saw the difference. He himself was involved because it was his job even though he was acting without a brief. But Zakayo was in it out of loyalty in a personal vendetta to square an account for a friend. Well, it took all sorts. One end, many motives.

Accra had a nimbus of light. Coming up out of soft tropical darkness, it was a fantastic city: soaring, high-rise apartments and tower cores for each precinct with spidery walkways running everywhichway like a random cast of paper streamers.

Chevron slowed and allowed Zakayo to pull past and run into the first parking lot in the suburbs. When he drew up Zakayo swung aboard, teeth catching the city lights like an open piano. "Okay Boss, straight on for the Metropolitan Throughway. The marina's half a kilometer out of town. That's where the Aqualife Club has its place. Keep it slow. You can do what you like when you get there; but security like you to stick to traffic regs on the way."

Accra was still quiet. It would be another two hours before its citizens recovered from the exertions of the day and moved out for a second bite at delight's cherry.

The park at the marina was four-fifths empty and Chevron picked his spot for easy getaway. It was a low, circular, two-floor building, rising in the center in a fluted column, with a revolving restaurant and observation lounge balanced two hundred meters off the deck. Higher again, a twin searchlight beam circled and dipped like a wobbly chopper.

Water surrounded it, opening on the far side by a short channel to a man-made lagoon which in turn had access to open sea.

Small craft lined the quays. Out in the lagoon, cabin cruisers, catamarans, vessels of every rig rode to multi-hued buoys.

A broad verandah with tables and a long continuous bar circled the lower floor. A few skindiving enthusiasts wearing black gear with brilliant red strips were still sitting about prolonging the late afternoon drink, so as to leave no thirsty gap before that and the late-night revel.

They crossed a swing footbridge over the moat and followed the verandah round until they were overlooking the lagoon. Chevron took an electronic stylus and wrote his name and hotel registration code on a disk for the Asian bartender. It was fed into a slot in the furniture, and there was a wait of fifteen seconds until it popped back and the man's Oriental mask could slip into drive and register a warm welcome.

"All clear, Mr. Chevron. Sorry to keep you waiting, but you know the regs for out-of-town clients. I hope you enjoy your visit. What can I get you now? Would you be wanting a reservation in the restaurant? There's a fine menu. You won't find better food on the coast."

"Just whisky and lime. All right, Zakayo?"

"That's fine for me, Boss."

They took their drinks to the rail. Zakayo had brought the okapi under his arm and stood it on a table like a mascot. Floodlights on pylons spaced round the mole turned the lagoon to bright day.

A cable-length out, a trim brown nude shot from the cabin hatch of a large white cruiser, ran lightly to the bow and paused with one hand on the flagstaff, looking back over her shoulder. A bearded character climbing more slowly pushed out to waist level waving a glass in a free hand. Dialogue was lost by distance, but her gesture was an international negative.

She balanced for a second like a figurehead on the stem directly above the nameplate *The Lotus,* dived cleanly with hardly a splash, then began a leisurely swim round the boat.

Nothing could be more peaceful: business as usual according to place and time. It was another illustration, if Chevron needed one, that the observed world was only the tip of the iceberg. Behind the façade, there was more going on than met the eye.

Even for the individual it was true all the time. What was said or done was only a fraction of the tale, a result of incredibly diverse forces, a compromise that concealed a long trail of experience and hidden suggestion.

Action, however, there had to be. Too much thought would bind his hands. He said, "Where does the club have its rooms?"

"Down below, Boss. There's an inlet tank. They can go straight out from the locker room into the lagoon. Only members of the club allowed in there."

Conviction grew in Chevron. It was an ideal setup. Ann Riley could well be here. After interrogation, she could be towed out and dumped in the sea, where piranha would do an identity erasure job at no charge.

Time was not on his side. They would go to work as soon as they could set up the gear. He moved along the rail looking down into the boats. Two up the line was a small cutter under bare poles, labeled *Devil Woman*

45

in Gothic script, moored by the stern to a ring bolt in the parapet. A man in a skin suit was half-in, half-out of the cabin, sorting through some small gear which he had tipped out of a fetch bag on the decking of the cockpit.

Chevron looked around. Everybody was busy doing his own thing. The girl in the lagoon had given up the hard-to-get gambit and was climbing back aboard the cruiser by the mooring chain. He said, "Give me twenty minutes. If I don't come back, go down into the locker room. Say you want to collect Dr. Poldano's belongings. Then play it by ear. Okay?"

"Just as you say, Boss."

Zakayo was all right. No questions. No arguments. Chevron waited for the barman to turn his back on a glass-polishing exercise and was over the barrier in a smooth vault.

He dropped with one foot either side of the man's head, steadied himself and went down to a full knee bend, chopping left and right into the sides of a bull neck. Going forward on hands and knees into the cabin, he reversed and hauled the body after him.

Zakayo had not moved. He was leaning on the rail sipping his drink, miming peace and contemplation for any passer.

Chevron ripped open the seals, peeled the suit off and climbed into it himself. Flappers, goggles and a neat lightweight breathing pack lay on the bunk. When he was set, he shifted back into the cockpit, transferred his blaster and a composite tool pack to an outside pouch, stuffed his own clothes into the empty canvas bag and pitched them up to Zakayo. Then he stood up, walked casually along the hatch coaming and dived into the lagoon.

Finning down, he touched a sandy bottom at five

meters. Overhead, the cutter was a dark bulge in a ridged aluminum roof. He swam slowly, under the hulls of moored craft, following the curve of the verandah wall. There was a sense of having moved out of his own time continuum, as though he had gone through a mirror to find that the images behind the surface had an independent life. It could have been five minutes or five hours before he saw what he was looking for: a gap in the craft overhead and a bright slick in the water coming from an opening in the wall itself.

Twenty meters inside, the entry port lost its roof and he was looking up from the floor of a circular tank with ladders every few meters round its circumference.

Chevron climbed into a locker room with a white tiled floor and banks of roomy lockers radiating out from the pool like spokes from a hub, each group identified by a letter code.

M/P was a fair bet and he went along reading the white ivorine tabs on each door. At the far end there was a ten-meter circulation space with chart tables, work benches to repair gear, issue bays for replacement air packs and beyond that shower rooms, club offices, a bar, a refectory and all the ancillary services.

There were not many people about. It was a good time. He turned the end of the bay, having progressed to O for O'Keefe and started down the other side back towards the pool.

Poldano's *pied a terre* was halfway down the line. Each club member had a meter-wide closet, running the full height of the furniture, a narrower set of six deep drawers. He tried the drawers first, feeling a way through the wards of the simple mechanical locks with a sensitive stylus from his miniature housebreakers's kit.

There was nothing, only the clutter of marine detritus that any diver would gather. They would be tipped out as junk by the next owner.

There was a point in that, if there had been time to think it through. You collected your quota of material which had value for you, but it didn't mean a blind thing to anybody else. When you were gone you were gone. Sunk without trace. The Norsemen had the right idea. Pile a man's possessions round him on the deck of a ship and let it burn.

Chevron turned his attention to the tall locker, freed the lock, paused with his hand on the catch to hear whether or not Zakayo was beating at the gate and then swung it back.

Ann Riley's wide-open eyes, startled by the sudden inrush of light, stared back at him over a white gag that covered the lower part of her face. Wrists were taped back at shoulder level to convenient coathooks. Ankles were bound together and wedged behind a strut, so that she would not be tempted to bruise her bare toes by kicking the panels. Other than the yashmack-gag, she was wearing minimal apricot briefs with the monogram AR worked in black in the left groin.

Chevron read it off, "A.R. You must be Ann Riley. What would you be doing hanging in there, then?"

Communication was not easy, but her eyes, adjusted to the light, managed to signal a whole raft of emotive response: relief that it was one of the home team; impatience to be off the hook; pique that he should be the one to be ahead in the balance of courtesies.

Chevron, busy with an unhitching chore, saw her problem and talked quietly. He said, "The Chinese have a word for it. It puts me 'on'; but don't give it a thought, I shan't claim any special privileges. Do you belong to this outfit?"

A near nude in a locker could never be entirely at ease; but he had hit the right tone. Some of the strain went out of her eyes and she nodded intelligently.

He lifted her out, screened by the open door, and turned her round to get at the knots behind her head. For a moment she leaned against him, skin smooth as alabaster, sandalwood pollen-cloud strength nine, and his fingers went suddenly clumsy.

When she could speak, she said, "How did you know I would be here? What are you going to do now?"

"That's two questions. Under one, I didn't know. It was somewhere to start looking. Under two, we get out. Do you have a suit?"

"Yes, in my locker."

"Okay, snap into it. Not that you don't look good the way you are, but we have to go out by the tank."

"I don't have the key."

It was true, the tiny apricot triangle had no pocket. Reading his mind she said tartly, "I didn't expect to be coming here tonight, if you remember."

"Okay, okay. Pull on that sweater in case we meet a bishop. I'll follow you."

In the few minutes it had taken, business had flourished. Each aisle had its quota of late returners. In the Q/R/S block there were half a dozen doors open. He came up behind her and opened the hatch. It was all very neat, everything handy and in its place, a tribute to an orderly mind. A virginal white molded suit was hanging at the back like a second prisoner.

There was not long to go before Zakayo would be starting off. He said, "Make it quick and follow me to the tank. If there's any problem, don't be reticent. Push a little cry."

"I'll do that. Though I can't help thinking the wolf is already on the sledge."

From the rim of the pool, Chevron could see between two blocks to the foot of twin ramps that connected with the upper floor.

Traffic was light and mainly going up. As he watched, a service trolley with a large oblong linen bin ran from the down lane. Two massive attendants, bare to the waist, complete with red tarboosh and lacking only the scimitar for the full flavor of Haroun's own eunuchs, stood together on the narrow footplate.

The nudge of a sixth sense shifted Chevron off his perch. When the wagon trail rolled directly for block M/P he was sure. She had been parked there temporarily, until the reception could be properly organized. Now they were ready and collection was under way.

They had it all sewn up. The Aqualife Club was a natural for an undercover group. Poldano was on to it, nothing more sure. His removal could be no more than a simple exercise in self-protection.

The trolley halted at Poldano's locker. One man threw back the lid of the container, the other was working on the lock. When the door came open, he took a step back. Dialogue was absorbed by the acoustics of the vault, but the mine suggested, "Abdul, the *bint* is no longer in the bin."

"You are a fool, Kazi. Among walnuts only the empty one speaks. Let me see."

"A stone from the hand of a friend is an apple. But she is surely gone."

"A-ah. You are right. We must advise the master. Call from the desk."

Ann Riley's voice broke into the reconstruction. She

50

said, "You surprise me, Mr. Chevron. I thought we were in a hurry."

It was on the formal side for one who had lately been chained naked to a rock and released by his hand, but he let it pass.

"That's so. The balloon is on the way up. Cover that mobile face with its mask and swim like any fish down the drain."

Zakayo checked his time disk and watched the second counter flip along for a full due. Twenty minutes the man said and twenty minutes it should be. He let the fifty-ninth marker slide to a double zero and left the rail, picking the okapi off its table and shoving it down the front of his shirt.

Three paces off his computer, catching up with the last visual data from the lagoon, sent out a warning pinger. There had been a twin-bubble trace from somewhere right of the cutter.

He went back. *Devil Woman's* truck was swaying with more than the light evening breeze.

A black and a white figure were climbing aboard from either beam. Teeth beaconing a welcome, he said, "Glad to see you, Boss."

"All quiet?"

"As the grave, Boss. The barman came over, asked where you were. I said you'd be right back."

A muted pinger from the bar had him round and moving across to be near the intercom point when the barman himself reached it. He heard the man answer. "No, Mr. Kruger. Sure, I'll call right away if I see her. There isn't a Caucasian woman dark or fair in this bar. There hasn't been one in yet this night. One stanger. A

Mr. Chevron. His friend's here at the bar now. Do you want to speak to him? Okay, I'll have him wait."

His smooth transition to the customer was a piece of public relations expertise. Without a change of expression at finding the party of the second part grinning at his elbow, he said, "That was the director, Mr. Labid. He thinks Mr. Chevron might like to join the club. He's coming up himself to talk to him. Your friend's lucky. We have a waiting list. Where is he anyway?"

"Looking at the boats. He'll be along."

"The director says to set up a drink on the house. Same again?"

"That'll be just fine. I'll go get him."

Chevron was already in shore rig. Ann Riley was out of sight in the cabin. Zakayo said, "The big man called up. The director no less. Called Labid. Wants to talk to you. He's on the way. Sent these."

"Check the bridge."

Zakayo put the glasses on a table and pushed off, miming a searcher's zeal. Ann Riley, a disembodied voice from the orlop said, "There's only one way out. They could easily close that. They have a big staff of bouncers. It's a very private organization."

He ducked his head through the hatch. She was closer than he expected, sitting at the nearer end of the starboard bunk with her feet drawn up to keep them away from the owner, who was still stretched out in the bilge.

Dark brown eyes, not half a meter off, considered him steadily. Whatever he had been about to say died the death. Then recall, triggered by the idea of a kneeling girl, superimposed an image of Paula beside his bed. He said harshly, "This is no time to sit on your elegant can. Root about in the lockers. Find something to wear."

Zakayo's husky rumble made a period. "Not good, Boss. They've got a squad there."

Chevron considered it. First close the door, then search the house. Not that much search was needed. It was known that he was there on the verandah, and without spraining his brain the director would guess that the girl would be close.

He said, "Okay. Over the top. Cast off as you come aboard."

At the same time, he swiveled a fishtail propulsion jet on its mounting in the transom.

Hot gas beat at the wall. *Devil Woman* strained at her mooring and Zakayo, watching his feet, sliced the rope with his knife. Chevron completed the arc and the auxiliary motor delivered its full thrust with the jet under water, churning up a boiling white wake.

The barman, seeing his client disappear as though by sleight of hand, whipped from behind his counter and crossed the floor. Four of the club's hatchet men appeared, two from either direction completing a pincer move round the circle to add weight to the director's invitation to a conference. They joined him at the rail. One peeled off hurriedly to make a sitrep. Two vaulted the rail and ran for the next boat in line.

It was a straight powerboat with triple jets, used for towing waterskiers. Zakayo said, "Not good, Boss. That bastard'll eat this skiff for breakfast."

The same thought had struck Chevron. They were half a cable out, making a steady seven knots with the auxiliary giving everything it had. He needed more power and a quick check round the lagoon showed the big white cruiser as the handiest source. It would disturb the personnel on board, but they would have to learn that every human activity had to take its place in the master plan.

Devil Woman surged alongside the cruiser as the powerboat shot from the quay. Chevron cut power, jumped for the coach roof and took off in a spring that carried him onto the higher deck. Zakayo grabbed for a passing bollard and braced his two feet against the transom. It was not seamanship, but the cutter had no choice. She lost way and slapped hard into the white hull.

In the best tradition of the sea, the owner put down his girl and his bottle in that order and ran for his bridge, enquiring earnestly of Allah for a full explanation. Chevron, preoccupied with an unfamiliar console, was no substitute for the All Wise and All Seeing; but he was the only one in sight, so the man repeated it, emphasizing his right by thumping the bent figure between the shoulderblades.

Chevron could see the powerboat creaming across the lagoon and reckoned there was no time for protocol. He spun on his heel, grabbed the wrist rising for another knock and wrapped it round the man's neck. Then he ran him to the open wing of the bridge and pivoted him over the rail into the sea.

Zakayo was aboard as the girl followed her captain, moving more slowly after her exertions, eyes wide and unfocused. He said, "Do you want this one, Boss?"

It was a tribute to a professional's dedication that Chevron could say, "No. Dump her."

Zakayo shrugged. Even the girl herself looked surprised and only recovered in time to make a good dive when he picked her up by crotch and neck, circled once and pitched her over the rail.

Chevron had sorted the angles. The hull throbbed with power. As Ann Riley came abroad he said, "Cast off."

Reactive time smartened by the action, she doubled to the bow, heaved over a patent release lever that dropped the mooring chain to its buoy and *The Lotus* took off as if booted up the rudder.

Craft rocked at their moorings. The long curve of the terrace was suddenly lined with a watching crowd. Men whose boats were handy jumped aboard and cast off. By the time Chevron reached the narrow strait to open sea, a flotilla was streaming into his turbulent wake. A chase is a chase is a chase. When one runs many follow. It was a nice object lesson for the house psychologist and she said bitterly, "They don't care. It's another game. They have a child's unthinking interest in living things, moving things, things of danger or of blood."

Chevron said, "Then we have to see that it isn't our blood."

He cut back power to take the channel with a concrete mole two meters off either beam. At the end of the fifty meter cut was a white blockhouse and a high gantry straddling the gap.

Zakayo said urgently, "The sluice. There's a lock gate, Boss. They close it and drain the lagoon once in a while."

Closer in, Chevron could see two men on the gantry behind a plexiglass dodger spinning a large wheel set horizontally on the decking. He said, "Take her along dead slow," and ran for the open wing of the bridge. Then he was on the mole and going for the blockhouse on a weaving course.

He reached it well ahead of the cruiser. Its double-leaf teak door was solid and he used his blaster to melt out the lock. Inside were a console along the sea wall, a video which Labid had used no doubt to alert the post, and a litter of marine gear. A companion up left led to the gantry and Chevron took it two rungs at a time.

Black feet appeared on the top step, together with the foreshortened figure of a man striking down with a boathook.

Chevron gripped with feet and knees and leaned back, feeling the vicious swish of air in his face as the hook sliced past with a centimeter tolerance. Then he had the shaft in a double grip and heaved.

Off balance, the striker could only follow his rod, and came down head first with Chevron swinging clear to give him sea room.

Up aloft, the second worker was still busy with his wheel. Chevron reversed his blaster and picked his spot for a neat, clinical blow that sprawled the man over the spokes in a slow spin.

A depth telltale showed the gate as half up with two meters of water still clear. The cruiser had nosed up to the gantry and Chevron called down, "Take her through. Slowly now. Be ready to go astern if she fouls."

The powerboat, still ahead of the field, was racing for the channel. As the cruiser slid clear, Chevron spun the wheel.

The powerboat entered the channel. Zakayo shouted, "Time to go, Boss."

With the gauge showing under a meter and the powerboat not fifteen meters off, Chevron sprayed a blast into the gear and locked it solid. Then he balanced on the gantry rail and took off for the cruiser.

Zakayo watched his feet hit the deck and fed in full power.

Chevron sprawled flat on his back. *The Lotus* picked up her foot and beat off into instant night and the long rollers of the open bay.

IV

THEY STOOD in line on the bridge, with only a small binnacle light to locate them in space and time. *The Lotus* drifted with only enough way to keep her heading into the sea. Ahead was more empty space than the mind could accept; astern Accra and its suburbs were an arch of variegated light.

Chevron, in the center, with Ann Riley at his left and Zakayo on his right, thought aloud for the benefit of all hands, "Taking this ship brings in the *gendarmerie*. But Labid won't want the good doctor here shooting off her mouth and telling all about being incarcerated in a locker in her gaudy pants. So he'd see that he got to us first. We all know too much for his peace of mind. It'll be a priority one operation. Neither of you are safe in Accra. So we have to find somewhere else."

There was silence, except for the run of water along the sides and a slap as *The Lotus* smacked at a long roller.

Ann Riley said, "It's hard to believe. Why should they want me? I've been working at the unit for two years and this is the first time I've been threatened. They could have got to me any time."

"It's that fickle finger. If you'd stayed in your own *gydda* combing your raven hair, you'd have been ignored. But you didn't and you weren't. There's no turning back the clock. Believe it, as of now, you're a marked woman."

"What will they think at the unit?"

"Not as much as they would have if your gnawed bones had drifted in among the surfers tomorrow morning."

"That's still a possibilty."

"No, they won't search any more, just yet. They'll let things quiet down. Labid'll talk to the owner. Sometime in the small hours, he'll send out a few company cars to sink us. They'll have a fix on this junk with infrared or straight sonar."

"So there was no point in all the violence and putting ourselves wrong with the law?"

"There's one very good point. We're all alive and able to argue the toss. That's always a big factor. Which reminds me that you could nip down into the galley and use those trained fingers to open a few cans. And coffee. Make some coffee."

It had been a confusing night for Ann Riley; but she was still in there pitching. "Why me? Why can't you do it for yourself?"

"Division of labor. There are those who have to think and those who have to hew wood and draw water. Go and do it."

Chevron ended on a tone that made it plain that he did not care either way whether he was liked or not.

Darkness hid her face, so he missed an expression which might have warned him that the score was noted and that if there were any ground glass in the cabin stores, he would get a heaped spoonful in his cup. The voice was on the tight side, but the form of the words was willing enough.

"All right. All right. I just like to know. Give me ten minutes."

When she had gone, Zakayo said, "She's taken it very well, Boss. A lot happened at once for her."

Unspoken was the suggestion that Chevron was being too hard.

"I know it. She hates my guts. That's a good thing.

58

Takes her mind off her troubles. Everybody needs an interest."

As he said it, Chevron wondered what his own was. Action for its own sake was not enough. Nor was irritation with the department and a desire to prove Wagener wrong on all counts. On that last, he was not doing too well at that. Going outside the brief had fouled it up properly.

That was something else. He was a danger now to the department. There was a third force interested in shutting him up. Labid and the regular security forces, he could identify; but if the word went out that he had gone solo, he would be hunted down.

Who would it be? Batista and Mosander were the nearest in Freetown. But more likely it would be one they knew he had never met.

Chevron said, "This cousin of yours. Who knows about the connection? Would they look for you there?"

"Nobody at the unit knows, Boss. The doctor knew. But I reckon he told nobody. It's not the same name. There's no reason for anybody to tie it up."

"It could be dangerous for him."

"He owes me a few favors. But there's just one thing."

"What's that, then?"

"How do we get there? The beach is floodlit for five kilometers. Also there's heavy surf. The marina's the only place to take a boat in. Except the port at Takoradi and they'll alert harbor security."

"I'll think about it."

Ann Riley's voice spoke from the console. "Come and get it."

She had rigged a hooded lamp and closed venetian blinds on all the cabin ports. There was a heavy bouquet

59

of freshly made coffee and the cabin table held crackers, cheese, fruit and a small ham. The cook had even found time to change into a trim housecoat of pearl white silk with *The Lotus* stenciled in black across the chest. Chevron might be 'on' in his Chinese fashion, but she was ahead in the small courtesies.

Credit where credit was due. He said, "Well done, Riley. You're the flower of the medical service."

She poured coffee balancing easily like a born sailor, then left them to it, taking her own beaker out of the circle of light and sitting on the edge of the starboard bunk.

They ate in silence. There was a stillness about the girl that drew Chevron's attention. Even when she moved to put her beaker on a locker, it was a relaxed movement. Neat economical gestures. Satisfying to the mind. She had the okapi beside her and picked it up, holding it on her lap by its forelegs.

Clearly she was thinking of Poldano, holding a private wake which closed everything else out.

Chevron had a sudden urge to hurt. He said curtly, "He's dead. You won't see him again. You should pitch that thing away. Let the dead bury their dead. What was he, your father figure?"

"That's not clever. It isn't even good sense. Human relationships are all there is. I understand that he's gone. But grief is important. If you don't know that, I'd be sorry for any person who thought much about you. There's a cycle and nostalgia is at the end of the swing like a followthrough. If you leave it out it's incomplete. Then you do have a problem."

"That's official? Straight from the analyst's couch?"

"You can sneer, but it doesn't alter the truth."

"And how long does this vigil go on? When can we expect to have your full attention?"

Goaded at last Ann Riley stood up, swung the okapi and pitched it for his head. Good reaction time saved him from a shrewd knock. The animal carried on, missing his left ear by a millimeter and thudded into the bulkhead.

There was a digestive silence broken by Poldano's voice coming from the deck like Hamlet's father.

Public response was a hundred percent. Ann Riley leaped to her feet and came near to cracking her skull on a coach roof beam. Zakayo could not go pale, but he managed an ashen gray and said piously, "Holy Mother of God!" Chevron, who had seen the body and reckoned he could judge between the quick and the dead, had his blaster out in a smooth sweep that knocked a can of tomato juice off the tabletop and quested round for a target.

The okapi with its four legs in the air looked long dead, but it was the source of the illusion. Poldano's ka was, speaking from it, with a tinny harmonic that could only come from electronic gear on the blink.

Ann Riley was kneeling beside it. Chevron said curtly, "Don't touch," and got a slow burn that should have withered him on his stalk.

Poldano had gotten stuck on a loop and said for the fourth time, "Hello Ann. If you find this you won't be seeing me again."

She was very still, raven hair falling forward to hide her face. *The Lotus* lurched and she had to steady herself with one hand on the bulkhead. The okapi rolled on its side and Poldano picked up the thread.

"Thank you for everything. All things come to an end, however, good bad or indifferent. There's a moral in that somewhere. One thing you can do for me. You might meet an old friend of mine. Name of Chevron. Don't be put off by his manner. He's not the awkward bastard he appears to be. Give him my regards. Ask him how he got on with Jack Beukes. Take him along to the Aqualife Club. I bequeath him my locker. The worst journey in the world for me takes me away from where you are. Give my thanks to Zakayo. He's been a good friend. He can take anything he likes from the bungalow. That wraps it up."

There was a whir and a click. Ann Riley's hands were centimeters off the smooth fur skin when Chevron brushed her aside.

There was a muffled thud from inside the carcass and acrid blue smoke spurted from its mouth and eyes. The performance was stricly unrepeatable; Poldano had shoved a destructor capsule in the circuit. If she had listened to the record on her pillow she would have got an eyeful of soot.

Zakayo said, "So he knew. He knew it was a dodgy mission. He should have let me go along. I asked him. I said, 'Take me along, Doc.' I knew he was worried."

Chevron said slowly, "He was meeting me. He'd a shrewd idea they were on to him and didn't want him passing on any ideas he had. Knowing him, I'd say they were in that message somewhere. He mentioned the Aqualife. Well, it's possible I might not have seen the connection. He had doubts about Beukes. That could be useful. What else was there?"

"Only the personal bits about the three of us, Boss. Nothing there."

Ann Riley said unexpectedly, "There is something. *The Worst Journey in the World* is the title of a book. We found it in the library at the unit. It's very old.

Early twentieth century. More a documentary than anything, about polar exploration. Some types made a fantastic journey to collect a king penguin's egg. When they
got it back nobody wanted to know. Chad said it was
typical."

Chevron considered it. There had been a war about
Jenkin's Ear; but it was unlikely that the hemispheres
would be tipped off their delicate balance by a penguin's
egg. If anything, it was a hint towards a *locale*. At
least it tied in with Poldano's interest in ice.

He said, "Thank you. You might have kept that to
yourself. I don't see anything in it as of now, but there
could be. If you're all ready we'll work on the next phase.
I don't fancy staying on this boat longer than we have to.
Labid might just be ready to send a night party out."

Zakayo looked alarmed. "You're surely not suggest-
ing we swim for it, Boss? We'd be eaten alive in these
waters."

"I'm banking on there being some kind of dinghy. I
reckon it wouldn't be picked up at this range. Look
around on deck."

Ann Riley found it in a locker on the bridge. It was
a small oblong package with a warning in red that it
should be kept dry and should be trailed in the sea by its
cord when needed for use.

The advice was sound on all counts. Ann Riley, finding
therapy in action, watched it bulk out like mushroom
growth in time-lapse photography and judged that any
reveler tipping her drink on it on the bridge would have
been off liquor for the rest of her natural life.

She walked it round to the stern and hitched it to the
rail, found a double-ended paddle and pitched it in with
nice judgement. Accra was still a blaze of light, though
the ship's chronometer was reading 0315. If Chevron was

right, Labid would be marshaling a strike force. There was not much time.

Chevron made a final check on the bridge. He increased speed by a fraction and set the auto pilot for a course that would bring *The Lotus* to a landfall at Abijan if she were allowed to get that far. Then he called Zakayo who was searching for negotiable assets in the cabin lockers.

There was not much. The owner had gone in for a collection of erotica which must have pushed his credit to the top. Eros might well be life, but it hardly rated in this instance as a survival kit. There was a handgun and a pack of charges. That and a couple of bottles of local gin were all that he finally brought up.

Chevron said, "Time to go, Zak."

"Well time, I'd say, Boss. I only hope they don't look any farther than this skiff."

"Even an assassin will not look for what he has already found."

At sea level, the coastline disappeared. A glow in the sky over Accra was a mark to steer by. *The Lotus* had been small enough, but in the raft they were suddenly aware of the nature of the sea as they fell astern with the cruiser moving off as a dark shadow into deeper darkness.

Chevron took the paddle and dug it deep. The coracle slewed sideways in a trough and dipped so that Ann Riley was suddenly above him in silhouette. They had enough problems without a task force searching them out.

After five minutes trial and error, he got the rhythm of it and made progress. The crew kept quiet. It was plain enough that it would be a long haul.

After half an hour Zakayo took a spell, teeth shining whitely in the gloom, and Chevron joined the girl in the stern seat.

She said, "They still haven't come. Perhaps we should have stayed aboard and gone all out for a port up the coast."

As if in response, a small cluster of firefly lights separated out from the horizon on the starboard quarter. Chevron hissed, "Down flat," and swept her off the molded seat into the bilge where a couple of centimeters of water was swilling uneasily about.

One arm clamped round her shoulders, he held her flat as the raft, losing way, tried to beat its maker's specification and show that it could turn over given the right encouragement.

Chevron rolled cautiously onto his back. A long swell lifted his head so that he could see out to the horizon. The cluster of lights had passed, but above the noises of the sea he could hear the withdrawing hum of the motors. Four or five at the least count.

Ann Riley started to ask a question and got a wet salty hand over her mouth.

She began to count and got to a hundred. Then there was a distant crackle like a long burst of static, followed by a thud. Flesh and blood could stand no more. She sank her teeth into the restraining hand and sat up.

A column of flame was rising from the surface of the sea and the firefly cluster had separated out into discrete, individual pinpoints of light circling round it. As she watched, they reformed and began to come back.

Chevron's hand was not needed to keep her quiet. She suddenly felt cold. It was an assassination, as the man said. Somebody had passed the word and the pilots had gone out and blasted *The Lotus* off the charts. They had not seen the crew. They did not know whether they were short or tall or dark or fair or good or evil. It was a callous disregard for every human value.

Chevron hissed in her ear, "So now you know. Bloody good in fact. They've made their error and that gives us a break. They should have gone down to look."

The cars were gone, absorbed in the shore lights. The raft edged in, a good kilometer outside the last suburban spread. Zakayo, taking a spell in the blunt bow, said, "Heavy surf here, Boss. She'll go ass over tip."

Chevron held on for fifty meters until the clumsy raft was swinging everywhichway and the thunder of breakers was a sonic wall, dead ahead. He had to shout to be understood. "Everybody out. See you on the beach."

Ann Riley dragged herself wearily to her feet, hesitated only fractionally, then went over the side in a neatly controlled dive. Zakayo, with a bundle hitched to a cord on his left wrist, simply stood up and jumped over the bow. Chevron found the release valve and ripped it from its seating.

The raft seemed to dissolve round him and sank away. With the luck they were having, it would drift out and never reach the shoreline to put its plastic finger on the escape route.

Roaring filled his ears. Strong swimmer though he was, he felt himself shoved down under a sliding hill of sea. There was time to think that here was the ironic twist—he had gotten so far to be ground into shingle. Then the pressure was coming off and he was wading through a welter of broken water against the suck of the undertow. Ahead there was a slight, paler shadow between himself and the distant pallor of sand. It was Ann Riley, reborn out of the sea, her white housecoat sleek as a second skin and her hair flattened to a back skullcap.

He paced her, two meters away, noise of passage

66

drowned out by the withdrawing roar of the surf. Even crotch deep in water, she was moving with a pleasant grace.

She was a considerable fragment for Poldano to shore against the ruins of time. But it was a mistake to be involved, it weakened judgement. If experience had any value, he was outside the reach of that. However, public relations had its place. He pushed up his pace and spoke directly into her wet ear. "Never a dull minute. Seabathing thrown in. You'll wonder what you did before I came into your life."

The first word, coming out of the dark, was enough to bring her to a halt and he had to fend off holding her shoulders.

She shook herself free and ploughed on without a reply.

With dry sand under her feet she made a practical move which made it clear enough that he had no place in her personal equation at all. She zipped out of the housecoat and began to wring it out. He was just so much beach furniture.

Out at sea there was a glowing dot. *The Lotus* had burned down to her marks and was ready to sink.

As Zakayo lumbered from the shallows trailing his package, the dot flicked out. He used his knife to cut the cord and passed out a bottle of gin. "I reckon that's it, Boss. We can take our time. Couldn't be better."

Ann Riley, given the courtesy of the first swig from the bottle, took leave to doubt it. She was tired, wet, confused, disillusioned at a deep level and unable to see any good in the situation at all. In the starlight the good samaritan could have handed her a bottle of pure water and she have sunk three fingers of it over her salty tongue before she would have recognized it as the work of man's hand.

Zakayo caught the jar skillfully as it fell and Chevron thumped her helpfully between the shoulderblades.

When she could speak she said wheezily, "Pavlov and McDougal protect a simple maid. What was that then?"

But it had its use. When Zakayo led o up the beach for the tree line, she followed like a zombie. Where rational argument would have had a hard row to hoe, the local snake sweat had cut all the corners. Like Ophelia she even managed to hum a few ragged snatches of song.

Zakayo's cousin Usamah was not one to show a wealthy face to the world. The adobe wall of his house was blank to the square with one small door. When Zakayo operated a simple mechanical pull, a cowbell jingled in the distance and a dog barked twice before a light sleeper could cuff it to silence.

There was a stage wait. Chevron prowled about checking the other houses. Ann Riley crossed to a small fountain in the center, sat on the low stone rim and swung her feet into the pool. Her head was still thumping to the rhythm of drumbeats that had seemed to follow them every step of the way.

It was a small square in the old part of the town where Arab influence was still a living tradition. Behind the closed doors others would be listening but they were not curious.

Zakayo rang again. A grille slid open at eye level in the door. A beam shifted heavily from its socket. They were in.

There was a further complicated sequence of narrow passages, spiral stairs within the thickness of massive walls, coolness and stillness as though they were penetrating a *mastaba,* then, for Ann Riley, the pay-off in a large cool room with a tesselation of blue and gold tiles, a massive four-poster bed with stalactite decoration of pomegranate clusters and a star map through Moorish arches.

It was sanctuary. She allowed a brown gentle girl with heavy bracelets at wrist and ankle and long black hair bound in a rope with a spiral of silver wire to peel off the battered housecoat and lead her to a sunken bath in an alcove.

The sequence hit a harmonic of childhood memories of ancient tales. There could be a prince with a scimitar materializing out of an unguent jar. But she knew the prince was dead. Only Chevron appeared briefly to say, "All right? Do you have all you need? Get some sleep and we'll sort out a line in the morning."

It was an anticlimax. The prince had changed into a frog. She turned her face into the pillow and went to sleep.

Chevron watched her for half a minute. He was getting to have an insight into what she was thinking. She was genuine about Poldano. She was in fact what he had in error believed Paula had been to himself. So it was possible.

Although there was no personal gain in it, that was an important piece of information for his computer. Human solidarity was possible. But to fall in with the Arabian decor: a man cannot make a wine cellar out of one raisin. He would need more evidence before he was convinced.

Usamah held to traditional ways in the family sector. Courtesy included Ann Riley in the breakfast circle, but she was the only female on the set.

There was coffee, fresh bread and a choice of fruit. She sat back and watched the three men and reckoned that if she had it on a tape nobody would believe it.

Zakayo was showing a new side. As a kinsman of the house, he was in part the host. From the polite deference given to him by Usamah, he was clearly regarded as a person of importance. From the conversation, he was a man of property. Poldano had never mentioned it. Perhaps it would have been news to him. On the other hand there had been a lot of Poldano's life she had not known about.

Chevron was surprising her also. He was going on about the decorative spirit of Moslem art. He was saying that the West had misunderstood the Koran and put out a distorted view that there was some prohibition which excluded the use of living things as material for the artist, but in fact they made lavish use of animal, floral and human forms in everyday decoration. Maybe the fact was that they were not used so much for their own sake as realistic representations, but their spirit was abstracted and simply enhanced the dreamlike richness of the imagery.

He went on to compliment Usamah on his good taste.

Usamah, older than Zakayo, a tall, thin man with almost pure Arab features, bowed from the waist and offered fruit on an enameled platter which was a case in point.

It was as good as a play and Ann Riley looked stealthily at her time disk to see how long they would be at it before anybody got down to the hard question of why they were there and where they would be doing.

It took thirty minutes by the clock and gave Chevron a new dimension. He could be patient and subtle and had a necklock on a whole raft of arcane detail about Islam. He might have been a special envoy from Allah the Compassionate his own self.

Usamah was obviously delighted and would have settled for a long visit at his own house but Chevron was against it.

"Can there be any generosity left other than that you have already shown us? But no. We must leave Accra altogether."

"Then I have the very place. Our company operates as far north as the Gambia. There is a small branch in Bathurst. A car came down from there two days ago and should be returned. I was hoping for a request to cover the return passage, but none has been made and they will require the car for their own purposes before the end of the week. You will be doing me a service if you will take it back. I will speak to the manager there. Until you are settled you can live in the suite above the depot. It is kept for emergency purposes. Sometimes for instance, a traveler will be arriving in the middle of the night and wishes to leave again in the early morning. It is very simple, you understand, but you are welcome to use it. Perhaps it would be convenient if you traveled as Mr. & Mrs. Carter. I have some documents made out in that name which were not required."

There was more in the same vein. Ann Riley reckoned it was unbelievable that any business was transacted at all in the Arab sector. But she knew that over the years they had gradually got all the non-state commuter services in their hands.

The answer to the paradox came when the final decision was made. Usamah might have been a long time getting round to it; but once the path of action was clear he moved fast enough. Five minutes after the last coffee cup was cleared, a long-range shuttle flying the yellow and green houseflag of the hire company was settling on a reinforced strip in the center courtyard.

Zakayo took the pilot seat and flipped through the

controls with professional speed. It was fully fueled and provisioned for a two-thousand-kilometer trip.

Usamah and some members of his household lined the verandah to see them off.

The patriarch himself had changed into city gear: a white tunic top with a round stiff collar, well-creased slacks and a brilliant red fez. Beside him, the girl who had looked after Ann was standing straight as a spear, still sticking to her basic costume of bright jewelry, but making a gesture towards mixed company with a minute triangle of embroidered metal cloth.

Usamah had one hand on her hip where nature had put an ideal curve to accommodate it and used the other for a courtly wave. Then they were rising over rooftop height and the car was swinging to pick up a course.

Zakayo followed the line they had taken to the square and Chevron slid open a port in the deck to study the ground.

It was an area of narrow streets, secluded squares and courtyards like the one they had left. Women were busy with chores that had been carried out there for centuries. There was an air of permanence and peace. It was a far remove from the frenetic activity that kept the two hemispheres in their delicate political balance.

Hitting his mood, Ann Riley said, "I expect you could find the same over most of Southern Hem. And if that's so, what's all the brouhaha? Who stirs it up and for why?"

She got a reply which she could have given herself. "Aggression is a deep-seated urge. You don't have to be frustrated to have it. However much the historians and the political boys rationalize it with labels, causes one-to-five and all that cock, it's there all the time in the subconscious. If Northern and Southern Hem didn't exist, people would invent something else. Maybe its healthier the

72

way it is. They can go into a ritual dance every now and then and feel threatened. The only casualties are people like Poldano. So long as it stays that way I guess we have a useful function."

Opportunity to say bitterly that the price was too high at that did not come. Chevron said suddenly, "Take us down, Zak. Over there by the cypress trees. Not too low."

What he had seen was a blue-and-white security shuttle and beyond it another. Police were out in force and were checking every house in the precinct.

It could be a coincidence, but Chevron had stayed alive so long by not believing in coincidence as a statistical probability.

Zakayo confirmed it. He said, "The drums, Boss. I tell you nothing happens in this man's country that doesn't get reported. We passed through tribal territory last night and the message went out. But they won't get any change out of Usamah. He is very deep and very devious that one."

Chevron said, "He can delay it, but they'll get around to it in time."

He had been on the run before, but in the past there had been an organization behind him ready to pull him out. This was something else.

Zakayo fed in more power and they cleared the last of the old quarter. Below them there was dense bush like a dark green sea.

V

HENRY WAGENER walked through the operations room in the Northern Hemisphere Special Services bunker for the third time in the morning shift, scattering depression by the double handful.

As Raquel Cunliffe said to her co-worker Andy Stafford, wriggling her neat can uneasily on its high stool, "It wouldn't be so bad if he actually *said* something. But he just *stares* from under his eyebrows and it makes me feel transparent."

"To a pure mind that would be no problem."

"There's no call to be *nasty*."

Her computer made a period, going off on a solo run and she harvested a tape from the output, holding it between finger and thumb as though the machine had given birth to a serpent.

She fed it deftly through a decode unit and considered the open text with even more distaste.

"It's another one."

"That's all right. Take it in to him. Have your transparent thing strength nine. That tabard gives you a head start—if head's the key word."

"You take it."

"Not a chance. Chivalry goes only so far. Female suffrage brings duties as well as rights. Beside, where's your sense of history? They always send a lush virgin to appease the god. Allowing a little here and there for progress, the principle is sound."

Once on the hoof, she marched off at a smart clip. It was a fair index of the strain in the dielectric that nobody whistled or paced her step with a rhythmic clap.

74

Wagener's outer door opened to her personal code card and she went through into an anteroom. Robot scanners confirmed that her only offensive weapon was a bouquet of "Reverie" and his voice sounded curtly from a speaker in the facing wall. "Come in."

He was still on his feet, pacing up and down a strip of blue carpet that ran ten meters from his executive console to the door. He swung round to face the news bearer. "Well?"

"You said to bring any more meteorological reports straight to you."

"I know what I said. What does it say?"

"It confirms yesterday's forecast. A mean drop of one degree Celsius. No decrease in hours of sunshine. No special solar activity noted. It's from the monitor. Not a direct report to this office."

The implication was clear enough. She didn't see that it was any of their business. Buried half a kilometer under ground level, they were insulated from a bit of bad weather. Also, with over two hundred operators in the field there was enough going on without turning the security complex into an amateur weather station.

"How old are you?"

"Twenty-three. Twenty-four on Friday *actually*."

"I hope you reach your birthday."

"Thank you, Controller." Moved by nervous reaction she went on, "You'd be welcome to come to my party."

Transparent as she was, it was clear that she was baffled by his angle. She was even more baffled when he said, "I might just do that. Thank you for the invitation. Did you ever know any June with a progressive temperature drop like this one and snow recorded as far south as Birmingham?"

"No, I neve did. But there's nothing *sinister* about that. There's been freak weather before."

"So there has. So there has. All right, Miss Cunliffe. Is there any report from Chevron?"

"Nothing, Controller. He is twenty-four hours overdue. Shall I try to raise him?"

"No, don't do that."

Wagener watched her out and paced some more over his hard-wearing carpet.

It brought no comfort. There was something going on and against all reason he had a hunch that the diabolical weather over northern Europe had something to do with it. But to suggest that Southern Hem could engineer anything on such a cosmic scale was ridiculous. All that was positive was that they seemed to have used it to advantage. Almost as if they expected it.

That could be better forecasting. But there was nothing to choose between the orbiting satellites which fed data to the central observatory in the neutral zone. It was an area where scientific cooperation still existed and detailed treaty obligations made it theoretically impossible for either side to sell short.

He stopped at a long display spread tagged with the name of every agent in the field. Twenty black flags were a constant reproach and so many knives in his gut.

Christchurch, Suva, Montevideo, Capetown, Durban, Hobart, all the most southerly of his long-established listening posts had folded up. What, if any, was the significance of that? Was it just that his opposite number in Brazilia had a tidy mind and was working a geographical sweep latitude by latitude?

In any event, it was humiliating. He was being outmaneuvered and he didn't like it. Quite apart from the fact that some good men had gone.

Also there was pressure from the politicians. They were asking for reports that he couldn't give.

Bringing the map up to date, he shifted Poldano's white nametag and replaced it by a black one. Then he took Chevron's, weighed it in his hand and finally switched it for a red.

It was routine and its significance was double-edged. Chevron could be at risk himself or he could be putting the department at risk.

In spite of the tough line he had taken with the man at his last personal interview, he could not accept the latter. Chevron's record had been too good until the last mission and there he had met a run of bad luck that could come to anybody. It all depended on what scars it had left. Quite apart from the obvious scar. Maybe he should have been kept out of the field for a longer spell at that.

A muted beep from the console brought him to a halt by the desk. It was another visitor. Identity flashed up on a wall screen showed it to be the birthday girl on another trip.

He signaled for "in" and watched her across the threshold moving well and looking nervous. "What is it, then?"

"There is a report from Mr. Chevron. Well, not *from* him, but about him. Mr. Cassidy has called in to say that he has seen him in Bathurst. Asks if he should make contact. He will call again in fifteen minutes."

"Put him through to me when he does."

Wagener spent his quarter-hour studying a sheaf of reports from weather satellites. Somewhere at the back of it was a linking strand. He would stake his judgement on that. But what it was made no move to leap out of the text. Like Chevron, he had no time for coincidence. But every last one of the inquiries on loss of personnel had come out with a clear verdict of death from misadventure

77

—natural causes of a kind. The only positive conclusion was that it was too tidy. There ought to have been one in so many where the inquest raised a doubt.

Deaths on meteorological stations; persistent deterioration in the weather pattern over a good slice of Northern Hem; a progressive knock-off of agents in the south; what about it then?

Cassidy's clipped voice from the desk speaker brought him out of the mental *cul de sac* he was in.

"Cassidy."

"Controller. What's this about Chevron?"

"Here in Bathurst, Controller. Checked in yesterday. Staying in a transit suite over the Cape-to-Cairo Hire Company office. Two companions. An African who used to work for Poldano and a girl—dark slim number. I believe I saw her with Poldano once. Do I contact?"

"Not at this time. But keep close. Chevron is overdue. I'd like to know what he's playing at. Could be he has a lead or could be he's had a brainstorm and gone solo. Has he ever met you?"

"Never."

"You're sure of that?"

"I'm sure."

"Stay close then. Any other comment?"

"I'd say they were on the run."

"Send somebody to Accra and find out why they left. Call direct to me next time."

"Check."

Ann Riley stood by a long observation window in the penthouse suite of the Cape-to-Cairo Hire Company and had a long view down the broad empty Metropolitan Way to the river frontage. Beyond that point, hazy with distance, was the low coastline of the opposite bank.

It was siesta time and there were not many takers for a stroll in the sun. Habit died hard. She had a panel swung open and it was not as hot as all that.

She said, "I can understand everybody taking a break in Accra. It can get to be like a steambath. But not here, this is a good climate. Temperate. All these sun blinds are out of place. I bet some twisty contractor sold them the idea to get trade."

It was all interesting stuff, a tribute to an inquiring mind, but it got nowhere at all. Zakayo was out on some ploy of his own, Chevron had a magazine cutting spread on a coffeetable top and was reading it for the second time. When he spoke, it was on his own tack, as if she had not spoken at all. "Query. Why did Poldano cut out this article and mark it up with a red pen?"

"I told you, he was impressed by that old *Worst Journey* book."

"So why would he underline bits about the causation of ice ages? Was he expecting to have to get his kamiks out and fix you in foxfur panties?"

"You're an interesting case, Chevron. Why do you have to be so aggressive?"

Chevron let it ride and pressed on with his research. "This bit seemed to bother him. He underlined it twice. I quote: 'Why should the Earth, once in a state of glaciation, with consequent increase in *albedo,* not so stay for an indefinite period?' end of quote. What do you make of that?"

The professional mind was a sucker for the appeal to reason. She could not stay long in a state of pique when there was missionary work to do among the ignorant and backward. "*Albedo*? That's whiteness. Reflective surface. That figures. Once the Earth was covered so far in ice, there'd be a big heat loss. Solar heat, instead of soaking

79

in, as if to a storage heater, would be reflected out into space. The ice would have that much more chance of becoming permanent. Good reasoning. What's the answer? Why does an ice age ever pass once it's gotten a toehold?"

She crossed from her window and leaned over the back of his chair.

Chevron felt an electrical tingle in the back of his head. For a brief spell, he had a clear picture of her face within centimeters of his left ear. A twist and a heave and he could bring her round across his knees.

With an effort which gave an edge to his voice, he closed that avenue to one of many possible futures and said, "I know what *albedo* is. I want to know why Poldano was interested. Farther on the theory gets the full treatment. According to this man, the cycle starts in the Antarctic. The steps go like this. Ice gets thicker over the South Pole by natural additions of snow. When it gets beyond a certain critical thickness, there's so much weight of ice that the pressure on the lowest layers is high enough to bring them to their pressure melting point. So there's a sudden flow of intensely cold water out from the base. Once it's out from under, pressure is released, so it can freeze again. This forms massive ice shelves going hundreds of kilometers out from the Antarctic Continent and as much as two hundred and fifty meters thick at the sea edge. All clear so far?"

"Very clear. You're doing a neat job of exposition for a hatchet man."

Chevron toyed with the idea that he might yet bring her across his lap and see how she reacted to having her neat can whacked. Being a psychologist, she would probably put it down to repressed sadism or some such. He went on, "Then there's this increase in *albedo*. The total heat coming in is reduced by about four percent. The action spreads to the northern ice gap. Water which once flowed from the north remains there as ice. Eventually, the northern ice sheet covers millions of square kilometers. Total *albedo* is increased again. Heat input is eight percent down. Temperature over the Earth is down by about six degrees Celsius. You have an ice age, woolly mammoths, the whole shooting match. There's also a rise in sea level because of the extra ice."

"That's odd."

"All in the text, I assure you."

"No, the sea level bit. I did hear talk at the beach about that. There's more depth of water in the marina than ever recorded. There was some talk of having to raise the sea wall. The club committee was asking for a grant from the Regional Projects Board to finance it."

She stretched a smooth arm over his shoulder and picked up the paper. Again there was a small electrical discharge. Then she moved off and Chevron was left with a sense of loss.

Back at her window, she completed a trained reader's chore of milking the article of its sense in a quick scan.

"There's no problem. It all corrects itself. The situation doesn't stay in balance. Ice flowing out is replaced by much colder ice, which doesn't melt under pressure. Outflow slows. The shelf then breaks up quicker than it's supplied from behind. Solar energy reheats the southern ocean. Water circulates again and that *albedo* decreases. Once that cycle starts, the ice age is in retreat and you get back to *status quo*."

"Beside which the Polar Scientific Stations at either pole have a brief to check ice levels and control growth rate by release of heat. They have atomic generator plants to do that."

"That isn't in this account. How do you know that?"

"Let's just say I know."

Ann Riley said suspiciously, "What are yu trying to sell me, then? What's all the argument about if you know the answer?"

"Who would profit from a new ice age?"

"Nobody. It would be a menace all around."

It was true. On the other hand, Poldano was not one to waste time. He had seen something in it which was enough to trigger off an alarm—but not enough to justify a report to Wagener, or there would have been a general alert to all agents to look for data.

Ann Riley brought the crumpled double sheet and dropped it on his table. She said, "All the evidence points to the fact that we're holding off a natural cycle. A small operating error by your friends at the Polar Scientific Station would account for present conditions. By all accounts they're having a very lousy summer in Europe. But there's nothing *sinister* in that. They'll correct it."

It was all true. The twenty-fourth century had it buttoned up. Nature in the raw had to call the technicians uncle. Even now the adjustments would be being made to redress the balance.

Chevron remembered the huge complex built in the permafrost at Ultima Thule. He had made a quick trip two years back to investigate a fellow agent who had been suspected of passing information. He never had gotten around to finding him. He must have been tipped off that the jig was up. Instead of waiting to be asked, he had walked out into the polar night and disappeared.

For the first time, that past incident lined up in his head with recent history on satellite N5. The girl Martinez had done the same thing. But then she was not under investigation. There was no direct parallel.

There was the subdued hum of an elevator homing on the outside landing and Chevron shifted round to face the door with his blaster cradled in his palm.

Ann Riley had a sudden insight into the psychology of the fugitive. For her money it was just Zakayo coming in; but to Chevron it was a potential danger. His reactions were those of a hunted animal. To some extent Poldano had been the same. There was a kinship between them. Some of the feeling for Poldano spilled over in a sudden sympathy. A whole lot could be forgiven in men who had to live that way.

A pinger set in the door went into spasm. Chevron nodded curtly for her to get it and some of the empathy faded. To act the part with any credit, she reckoned she ought to be blonde, wearing an apricot negligee and buffing a freshly manicured nail.

It was a concertina door and when she slid it away there was a moment of anticlimax. It was not Zakayo and it was not the spearhead of a posse. A small man with a mild round face and rimless glasses was standing on the mat. He was wearing a white linen bush jacket, shorts, knee-length socks and brown sandals and had the greeny pallor under his tan of one who had seen long service on the coast. A salesman's grip was on the deck beside his left foot.

The hostess said, "Yes?" which was no big lead; but it didn't bother him. He said, "Nobody can mind their own business in this man's town. I was told there were some people staying over for a few days and I thought I might interest you in a few things."

"Such as what?"

"Such as almost anything. For a start if you're thinking of a safari over into the Sudan which is one of the chief reasons for anybody calling at this place, I can fix it. No trouble to your good self. Everything laid on. Perhaps I could come in and give you some idea of what can be arranged?"

Ann Riley said, "I don't think we had anything like that in mind."

Unexpectedly Chevron called across. "That's all right, dear. Let him come in. We might take a trip at that."

"You won't get better terms from any operator on the coast." The man was two meters inside the door and moving confidently for a chair by the table. "Cassidy's my name. I've been out here more years than I like to think about. But I promise myself after one more tour I'll pack up and go back to England. Wirral City's my place. Do you know that part? Mind you, with the weather they're getting as of now, we're lucky to be here. Nice climate this, when you get used to it. I guess when the time comes I'll have to think very hard about it."

Chevron had a moment of self-pity. He had drawn another Beukes in life's lottery.

He had shoved the blaster back in his waistband, but he kept his hand on the butt as Cassidy settled in his chair and undipped his portfolio.

But except for brochures, it was clean as a hound's tooth. Cassidy obligingly tilted it his way as he slipped out a handful and fanned them out on the tabletop.

The name of the agency was printed on every last one in thirty-six point Dorchester script: *Solar Vac Inc* with J. J. Cassidy, West Coast Agent, underneath in a bracket.

It was all true, like the man said and not a doubt, but it would be confirmed if he picked up the video and called the reference.

Chevron watched Cassidy's face and said, "That's

smart business. You only just caught us. My wife and I were planning to move on, today or tomorrow."

"That would be a pity Mr. . . .?"

"Carter. Mark Carter."

"Mr. Carter. Having come so far you ought to see what the region has to offer. You'd be surprised, I guarantee, at the primitive way of life that still exists in the desert areas. They hold on to their old ways. Stone-age economy. You'd hardly credit it could survive into this century. There's also been extensive restoration of prehistory sites. There was a flourishing culture at one time where now there's only desert. Makes you think. We just go around in a big circle."

Chevron stood up; enough was enough. "I'll think about it. Leave the literature." When Cassidy was at the door, he went on: "How soon can you fix a trip if I decide?"

"Give me six hours. That's all I need. What does Mrs. Carter think? If I might say so, she looks just the type to be interested in an unusual experience."

Ann Riley said, "Oh, I leave decisions like that to Mark. After all he has to pay the check. But we'll certainly consider it."

When Cassidy had gone, Chevron said, "Well done. You dropped into the part like a natural. Somebody is missing out on a very obedient wife with the right ideas about who pays the rent."

"Don't be too sure. I'm a professional type."

"What did you make of Cassidy?"

"What is there to make of him?" A nice, pushy little man."

"Could be. Too pat on cue for my liking. Still there might be something useful there. Drop out of the scene for a few weeks and play it by ear."

Discontent was stirring in the *Hausfrau*. "I've been thinking about that. Don't think I'm not grateful to be plucked from the slaver's hand, but looking at it in the light of day, I don't see that I have to go on running. This is the twenty-fourth century. We do have law enforcement. Why can't I stay here for a time, then report to the Regional Security Office? Maybe I shouldn't go back to Accra, but the contract period was due to terminate anyway next month. I don't have to renew. I could go back home."

"Sadder but wiser."

"Wiser."

Chevron considered it. She had a point. It was just possible that Southern Hem would leave it there. They were not out to take unnecessary risks. She was not important enough for a long-term vendetta. On the other hand, some careful depositions would have been made in Accra. The affair at the Aqualife Club would now be rigged to look like some kind of drunken junket. There could be charges lined up that would ensure that she was returned to Accra in irons without an option. Also, it would put the finger on the route he had taken.

Every issue has its complication of self-interest, but he believed he had discounted that when he said slowly, "It's not so simple. They don't give up. If you report anywhere on the west coast you could be taken back to Accra."

"Well, we can't stay here forever."

"I want to drop out for a while. I'll travel north. I might as well take you out of this territory. If we cross the border into the North African Federation, they can't touch you on a civil charge. You can make arrangements from there."

"Take Cassidy up on his offer?"

Chevron was saved a reply by a smart rap on the fancy door. He reckoned if he settled in he would need an early warning system. Whoever it was had bypassed the elevator and made a long quiet climb.

Before Ann Riley could do her suave Abigail bit, the door was open and Zakayo was filling the space. There was beaded sweat on his massive forehead and the smile was more a rictus of effort than anything, but he was alone.

Chevron said mildly, "Don't do it, Zak. You came very near to having a needle beam right through that dark shiny skull."

"Trouble, Boss. I have a cousin in Security. He tells me the local controller has applied for a warrant to hold you and Miss Riley. They'll have it before the end of the afternoon. It has to be signed by a circuit judge and the nearest is in Dakar."

Chevron said to Ann Riley, "That's your answer. You'd be back in Accra before tomorrow's light. They'd make something stick. If it ever came to court. On house arrest you'd be sitting duck for Labid's boys. Suicide of nubile medic unable to face disgrace of sentence."

As he said it, the nudge of a sixth sense told him that he had short-cirucited a whole raft of analysis and gotten smack on a truth. Suicide *was* their weapon. It put a new slant on the Martinez case. In spite of everything she had been got at in some way.

But it raised another question just as difficult. *Why,* for God's sake? There was no more inoffensive operator in the meteorology service.

Zakayo was waiting for executive action. Having said that the Hun was at the gate, he expected the garrison to leap up and down. He said, "There isn't much time, Boss, they could move first and wait for the order. They're sure to get it."

The pamphlets were still spread on the table. Chevron swept them together and read off the top one. "See the noble Tuareq who covers his face before women and strangers. Let the stars point your way in the trackless wastes. See the caravans that still ply their ancient trade across a wilderness that stuns the mind."

It was a tough choice. Ann Riley had a suspicion that she would be better off in an air-conditioned brig with three regular meals. But then she might also be dead. Most trips would be better than that. She voted with her feet, moving to her bedroom to collect her new toothbrush.

Wagener was still at his console when the priority link beeped for a direct personal call from an agent on the twelve degree band. He reckoned it would be Cassidy and he was not wrong.

"Wagener."

"Cassidy reporting direct."

"Go ahead."

"There was trouble in Accra. Poldano's bungalow was burned out. The girl must have been involved. She left with Chevron. I believe she was in danger. I'd say Poldano was onto something and they thought she might give them a lead. Chevron took a boat from the harbor, which disappeared without trace. I'd say he was keeping the girl out of harm's way. He came here in a hire shuttle, but the heat's on. He's contracted for a fifteen day safari, paid double for quick and discreet service; but that's okay. They can't go far out of line in a sand crab. To make sure, I'll go along myself."

"Do that. I don't have to tell you to watch yourself. Chevron's dangerous, make no mistake. I'm still hoping he'll see sense and call in with an explanation. But he went through a bad patch. Judgement rattled. I leave it to you to decide if you think he's a menace to the organization."

"Check."

Henry Wagener had had enough.

A precept from a training manual came into his head: "When in doubt, cue in the subconscious. Relax. Do something different. The problem-solving mechanisms in the mind will be released to shift around and try a new angle."

He called the outer office. "Controller. I shall be out for two hours. Call my personal link for anything above a two star."

A second exit behind the desk with its own scanning gear monitored him out. Suit texture, contents of his pockets and his physiometircs down to a mole on his left wrist were recorded and filed with a thousand others in the holographic memory bank. Over the years it had got his blueprint to a fine tolerance.

As the elevator whisked him through the onion layers of the Earth's crust, he speculated about it. There was a kind of immortality there. He could even imagine his alter ego stepping out of the box and taking over his chair. It was welcome.

The elevator stopped and a video gave him a scan of the scene outside. It was a busy monorail terminus. He was in the end slot of a row of a dozen elevators, but without direct access. He tuned for a picture of the next cage in line and waited for it to empty. Then he operated a pushbutton sequence which closed its door on the heels of the last commuter and rolled back a narrow panel in its adjacent side. His own cage opened a matching panel and he stepped across.

Once inside, he pressed a stud on the face of his time disk and the console responded on automatic. Five seconds later he was stepping out into the lobby as though he had just arrived fresh from the street above.

A tall, oblong hover truck with an attendant in the all-white garb of the city cleansing department threaded its way through the crowd and veered alongside, while its operator leaned off his platform to use a suction hose on a discarded cigarette pack.

Wagener had been neatly isolated from the press with the stern of the machine swinging to block his onward path. He stood still waiting for it to pass, one hand fending off its slab side. Daily custom had dulled any sense of menace. He thought irritably, however, that he would put in a memo that trash collection should be limited to off-peak hours.

The thought was hardly out of its hole when the middle section of the container whipped smartly aside and four hands took him in a comprehensive grip.

Sure in the knowledge that a security satrap would have some very refined gadgetry about him, the two men who flattened him on a thin mattress of trash gave no degrees of freedom whatsoever for any signaling ploy. Wrists and ankles were taped out in a taut cross. A soft foam plug on an adhesive strap closed his mouth.

Vision was still strength nine. Unlike Raquel, it caused his eyes no discomfort. He was therefore able to see that the interior of the box had been substantially modified for its special use. There was a large scanner in the roof giving a picture of the set. There was no panic. The man at the tiller was taking it slowly, stopping now and then to lift an unconsidered trifle with his nozzle. A fine stream

of dust settled on Wagener's indestructible metal-cloth city
suit. Nobody had noticed that one of their number had
sidestepped out of the action.

A man with a polished shaven head was in focus and
spoke quietly to his partner who was out of sight behind
Wagener's head. "For God's sake tell Harry to stop that.
Dust brings on my hay fever. I'll be sneezing all night.
Do you know that? I've got a allegory."

On the scanner, Wagener saw the pilot shove his hose
in a clip and shift over to his console. A voice behind him
said, "Okay, Harry, wrap it up. Straight for the disposal
bay."

It was all too easy. The truck increased speed, turned
right into a freight ramp with its motor dropping a tone
as it climbed for the daylight. At the top it checked, waiting for a place in a stream of hirecars, then moved along
the service lane for a hundred meters until it could peel
off into a delivery-and-dispatch area.

Harry maneuvered alongside a waiting truck, which
swung out a couple of grab arms to lift the container off
its chassis and swing it on board.

As soon as it touched down, they were away, with a
different rhythm—wheels this time, pounding the metalled
roadway.

The bald man switched the scanner out and Wagener
was left with the sense of movement, which he reckoned
was around twenty kilometers per hour, and a sense of
time, which clocked up around seven or eight minutes,
before the truck slowed to a halt, moved on down a slope
and finally stopped altogether.

They were there. Wherever there was.

When the trick panel slid away again, there was a lot
of light. Wagener reckoned it was a subway below one of
the tower blocks, lit by roof ports.

Beside the truck, two fingers in white with gauze face-masks reached in and bundled him expertly on a hospital trolley. A needle jabbed sharply into his left shoulder and the scene dissolved into black night.

VI

ANN RILEY watched the fire of realistic stick simulates blossom like a red desert flower in the center of the *laager* and left the circle to look at the desert. She rounded the bluff bows of the sand cat and found a seat on a guard fender designed to stop any excited traveler from falling from the cab into its broad caterpillar track.

The machine was a personal acoustic cowl and the small noises of making camp were cut off. Looking straight out she could imagine she was alone. For the first time in years, she was seeing the sky as something other than a filler of odd gaps in a visual composition. It was an inverted bowl. A black inverted bowl with small brilliant holes as though there were unimaginable light behind it, altogether bigger and higher than memory had recorded.

Although used to the idea that all places were accessible, they were usually so much alike that the mind had no sense of change. Give or take a few details Accra or London or Washington D.C. had more in common than they had apart. One tower block in a synthesized metropolis was interchangeable with another. But this was something else.

Cassidy had certainly fulfilled every claim in his brochure and exceeded a few. Rapid calls to his expedition center at Oualata had established that there was a small unit fresh in from a trip and ready to go. Taking a personal interest in the best traditions of the service, he had flown them out in his own jet.

When they arrived at the road head, the transport was tanked up and ready to go: a large sand cat, with meter-wide sponge plastic treads and two scout tenders with flight potential for observation, fall-back secutiry, or as excursion modules to interesting sites.

At the last minute Cassidy had carried courtesy beyond the call of duty and said he would go along himself to make sure they missed no nuance of the desert life. Now they were a hundred and fifty kilometers into the outback, moving due west on a line that would take them to Timbuktu.

Although the fiber-sheathed skin of the sand cat was still warm from the day's heat, the night air was cold. That was surprising in itself, because she had thought of a desert as being uniformly hot.

It was a limbo. The past was dead. She had a moment of insight into what it would have been like in Accra. She would have been miserable. It would have taken a long time to adjust. But the break had been brutally complete. She felt that she was just recovering from post-operative shock. Any bridges ahead could be crossed when she came to them. They could not indeed be crossed at any other time.

Chevron's voice in her ear cued in the present. It said, "If you're going to stay out there any length of time you'll need a sweater."

He had come round the stern of the cat and gotten within a pace without making a sound.

"Your concern for the ship's company does you credit. A new side to the iron man."

"The desert brings out the *sheikh* in me, beside I don't want to be held up by a female with an ague."

"You could be right. This *sheikheit* doesn't go so far as actually going to get it for me?"

"It does not."

"Right. I'll be back."

Chevron took up her niche and considered the desert for himself. There was a doubt needling the back of his mind and the empty canvas did nothing to distract it.

The operation had been so smooth it just wasn't true. Cassidy had gotten them out of Bathurst as though he had been running an undercover escape route as a profession. Perhaps that was the angle that made Solar Vac Inc pay dividends. Anytime now he might put the bite on and ask for his bonus.

But he had done it all without question, making no comment on a shopping list of personal gear which proved conclusively enough that he was dealing with people who traveled suspiciously light. Any normal operator would have wanted more collateral.

Chevron walked a few paces out and gave himself a cigarette. There was certainly an atmosphere. The company pennant was flying from an aerial mast above the cat's plexiglass canopy, streaming gallantly in the draught of the innr-change exhaust flue. All that was missing was a column of legionnaires stumbling over a dune singing the Marseillaise with parched, cracked voices.

Fantasy took a knock when a finger touched lightly in the center of his back. Reaction was basic and uncluttered by thought. To Ann Riley the discreet signal seemed to trigger off an explosion as though she had pressed a button on a demolition job.

She found herself flat on her back, legs in a scissor grip and her head grinding its own hollow in the eternal sand. Too surprised for an "eek", she could only glare into Chevron's face and strain pneumatically against his blanketing weight. It was getting to be a regular sequence.

Tactile clues told him that he had taken caution too far. He took his hand from her mouth and was surprised himself when she said, "Shsh."

But it was not an invitation to carry on and keep it quiet. She went on in an urgent whisper: "Quickly, something you should see."

He rolled clear and she was on her feet without waiting for a helping hand, moving back the way she had come.

Flames from the small fire lit the triangular space between the three vehicles. Zakayo and the six Arab drivers had set up a barbecue and laid out a long table with folding chairs and a canopy. Cassidy was nowhere in sight.

Ann Riley pointed to the top deck of the cat and went up the outside ladder on silent feet. The observation module was a single open space under the plexiglass dome with Pullman comfort in the shape of individual easy-chairs and a drinks dispenser console in the stern.

She had been sitting in the bow, where the glass bubble ended two meters short of the full length of the lower deck. Below that point was the cockpit and the deck head was pierced by a succession of ventilation louvers.

She knelt down by the chair as when she'd picked up her sweater from a locker under the seat and Chevron went down beside her.

Excited by the action, she was sending out a warm female bouquet and he felt the electric tension build in his head. But the scene below brought in the cognitive channels strength nine and left nothing over for eros.

Cassidy was just in sight through two louvers. He was set up in vision by a pilot lamp over the console. Even from the back of his head it was plain that he was intent and serious. He was talking to somebody, but he was not using the video on the communication spread.

He seemed to be speaking into his right hand. Then

he put his hand to his ear with something cupped in the palm.

Chevron had done it too often himself to be in any doubt. His own communicator was snugged in a belt pouch against his groin. He patted the girl's arm, partly in congratulation and partly as a signal to move out before Cassidy had finished his chore. They would be discovered eating *kebabs* with the *hoi polloi*.

The midnight hour seemed to have put an extra edge on Wagener's voice. Also the old bastard appeared to be losing his mind. He had said he wanted to know the score and yet, in the event, he had asked why he was being bothered at that time with a routine report.

Cassidy could imagine that much of it, from all quarters of the globe, could mean that the Special Services chief would be disturbed every half-hour through the night. But then, if he didn't want it, he shouldn't ask for it. He also seemed to have forgotten the detail about Chevron. When reminded, he had said, "It is too dangerous to let him go on alone. Arrange an accident. Also his companions. It should be easy enough. You will not have the means to get any information out of Chevron, but you might try the girl. It is possible that she would know if there is anything behind his movements other than random reaction to circumstances."

It was fair enough. But it was a turnaround from the previous position, where he was ready to give long service in bad stations a break.

From what he had seen of Chevron so far, Cassidy was inclined to·believe that he had gotten involved in a chain reaction after Poldano's death and had not deliberately cut himself off the link. But the result could be the same for the service. If he was picked up by Southern Hem, damage would be done before it could be stopped. Wagener had the right of it. It was common sense. But the old sod might have sounded as though he regretted it.

If he could have seen Wagener, he would have realized that any positive emotion was at a premium.

Henry Wagener had a conscious sense that he still lived at some deep level where electrodes could not probe, but having said that he had said all. Not that he was worried. Relaxing drugs, shuffling around his synapses, had left him full of calm and wide open to the world. He was in a small private room in the experimental wing of the city medicenter, lying on a narrow trundle bed and hooked up through a multicircuit skullcap to a complex computer spread which analyzed mental activity as soon as it formed a thought in its holographic womb.

Earlier, he had watched without any emotion when his very twin had dressed carefully in his discarded clothes and prepared to take up the action where he had left off. Obviously it was a long-laid plan. The man was already well-briefed. They had gone over a number of points, habits, names, current work in the section and the details he had given had mainly confirmed what was already known.

Perhaps deep down in that still center where he lived, there was a current of unease. But on the surface, tapped by the busy electronic gear, there was only willingness to oblige and frank answers to all questions. The biological machinery had been outsmarted. Even the will to bite into his left wrist for the oblivion pill in its capsule under the skin was gone. For that matter, strapped as he was, he couldn't reach it. But even the thought was outside the scope of his bemused head.

Before taking up residence in Wagener's solitary pent-house flat which capped the Watergate tower block of Chester City, Wagener II had put in a short stint at his office.

Confidence in the operation had been well-placed. It went like a bomb. The high command had been right all along the line. With his solitary habits and the whole nature of his organization, the top man was a natural for takeover. He would have been less sure if he could have seen the honest doubt in the checking gear which mon-itored him in.

There was a delay of ten seconds before it gave a con-ditional clear and released the locking mechanism for the inner door. In that time, it had run a second scan. Ninety-nine point nine of the two thousand physiometric readings were within the tolerance, but brain electrical pattern was fractionally out, on the negative side.

The delay sent a small surge of apprehension along the circuits and the second scan had a boosted reading. Taking the average, the machine gave him the benefit of the doubt and he was over the threshold of acceptance.

The new data went on the profile, coded into the slowly changing norm.

Next time it would be okay. He would be in with a mar-gin.

Carefully trained for the exercise, Wagener II spent an hour getting acquainted with the office hardware. It was basically the same as that used in Brazilia. Some not so good, some with refinements that they would do well to copy. Not that the North would be any threat in the years to come. Once the operation got under way total disruption would set her back for a millenium.

The thought was enough to trigger a mild euphoria.

Raquel Cunliffe, that busy messenger, reported back to the factory floor that he had given her a very *sinister* smile.

Stafford said that it was the invitation to the party and that it had been taken as the green light and she would have to watch it.

A sensitive barometer to male interest, she said, "He seemed *different*. Not so *penetrating*."

"Lulling you into a false sense of security. But never fear. If he gets you in a corner with a Bloody Mary, just raise your Ebenezer and I'll be right behind you."

"I don't think I have an *Ebenezer*."

"Every girl should have one."

"He didn't mention the party *actually*. I think he's forgotten."

Wagener II left by the public exit, appearing in the operations room a few minutes before the change of duty personnel and watching the procedure through the scanning lock before joining the queue.

It was all too easy. Wagener was obviously not noted for small talk and could be expected to stand in the elevator for the whole upward trip without exchanging more than a nod. He was beginning to enjoy it. The thought crossed his mind that it was a pity they were moving into the end game. He could have spent a year or two in the top slot. It was the sort of promotion he was not likely to get in his own group. Indeed, five years older than the man he was replacing, he had definitely missed the executive desk which would have capped a thirty-five year stint in the false beard business. Still, he would not do badly out of it. The years of preparation had borne the fruit. It was a last mission. There was a *hacienda* outside Sao Simao which had already been purchased in his name, with a pension double what he could have expected in the ordinary run of the service. It was all happening for him. If Raquel had met him on the subway, she would have reckoned that there was Latin sunshine in the Wagener depths.

Which was more than could be said for the weather in the streets. The sky was uniformly gray and overcast. A cold gusty wind blew from the river. The city heating engineers who relied on a seasonal drop in demand to do essential maintenance on installations were faced with normal winter peak consumption. People were staying home, turning up the heat and watching old programs on their actualizers.

Lack of heat was no problem for Cassidy's caravan. Pushing on at a steady fifty kilometers per hour, with a dawn start, he took the midday halt within an hour of Timbuktu itself.

The cat traveled well, with the two scout cars as out-riders raising a local sandstorm that persisted as a brown fan unfolding back to the horizon.

It was hotter under the canopy than in the cat, but Cassidy insisted on the ritual. It was all part of getting the feel of the environment and he didn't want customers of Solar Vac Inc to miss out on any collateral benefits.

Chevron was taking a professional's interest in the act. It was all first class. Withut Ann Riley's piece of obser-vation, he would have been taking it at face value, all criticism clubbed by the brilliant light and the stupefying heat. As it was, he was watching for a move that would give him some clue as to what Wagener had said on his late late transmission.

As a house delicacy, the cook served up a beaker of the regional nomad's dish to be taken when walking beside a camel: water, pounded dried goat's cheese and millet. All at blood heat, it was a sensation rather than a taste and one Chevron could have done without. But he could concede it would make a talking point.

Nutritionally it probably outranked the regular food that followed it out of the cat's well-found galley, basic staples realistically molded into cutlets with two veg and an iced *Bombe a la Tuareq.*

Cassidy's gambit was so innocent that it slipped by in the digestive chat.

He said they had a choice. They could continue east and make for Agades, then follow the ancient salt route across to Bilma, or they could head north for Taodeni, where there were a fertile crescent and an interesting surviving culture. Or perhaps they would like to go up in a scout car, circle round a bit and choose their poison.

The ball was in their court and even the psychologist fell for an open-ended situation. Chevron said, "Okay. We'll do that." He reckoned that a conference away from the caravan would be no bad thing.

Cassidy patted his mouth with his napkin in finicky regard for the niceties, swigged off the last of his hock and went off casually to check that the car was fueled for a solo trip. When they were all set, he said, "Take your time. The more days the more dollars. This reference is keyed on the auto pilot. It'll bring you right back whenever you feel the call for home. It's surprising what there is to see even in an empty quarter."

He waved them out of sight, unflagging in the call of duty, standing in the electric heat beside the cat like a fond parent.

Zakayo said, "He takes a chance, boss. Who's to say we won't take the car over the border? He's a very nice, trusting fella."

Busy at the console, Chevron let it go. On the face of it

that was the way it was. He hoped Ann Riley would not put in a qualifying gloss about their host's less frank and open habits.

She did not. She was learning fast. She left it to Chevron and was noncommital. "This trip was a good idea. I'm beginning to enjoy it. Where do we go then? What about northeast? There's a range of hills that way. But is it too far? What's the scale on the chart?"

Chevron was sidetracked by the smooth finger stubbing at the navigation spread. As a symbolic part for the whole, it stood in very well for its owner. Supple, efficient-looking, with a trim oval nail, he was moved to take a bite at it, but there was other material claiming priority in his computer. He said shortly, "Why not? Let's take a look," and fed the course to the flight selector gear.

For thirty minutes he pushed the car hard at its ceiling, just below mach 1, and the foothills of a long range pushed up as a smudge on the horizon. The character of the foreground began to change. There were tracts dotted with scrawny acacia.

Chevron cut back speed and dropped to five meters, with the car's shadow hard-edged on the ground. Seen close, a series of hummocky crescents were identifiable as the work of man. He killed forward thrust and drifted down in a local sandstorm of dust and small trash.

Ann Riley, about to ask the obvious question, got a mimed request for silence and a clear instruction to bale out and save it for later. Zakayo was already unsealing the hatch and had it back as the car sidled to a stop with its skids just clear of the ground.

Heat fanned in as though from an open furnace door, beating the airconditioning plant which ran to its red quadrant for maximum delivery.

Chevron, last out, threw down a candy-striped wind

break with light duralumin support rods and the food pack which Cassidy had put in with his own thoughtful hand.

It was not until he was twenty meters from the car that he spoke to his puzzled crew and Ann Riley was ready to club him with any handy fossil log. He said, "Over the wall into the next crescent."

"Can I ask why?"

"You can and when we're there I'll tell you."

Since it was all she was going to get, she climbed the jagged heap of rubble and waited for the oracle on the outside of the crescent.

At one time the walls must have stood five or six meters high, giving shade and a solid barrier against the Harmattan winds. Even now there was more sense of exposure to the primitive desert outside the barrier. It was a crazy *venue* for a picnic.

Chevron said, "I could be wrong, but anything we say in the car could be on transmission. It would take too long to find the pickup. The question is, do we stay with Cassidy or do we take this free offer and make a break?"

Zakayo said, "I've watched him, Boss. He's no fool. He wouldn't stay in business if he didn't have some safeguards. What's the angle? How does he stop people doing just that?"

"That bothers me. With six men along, you'd expect him to send one with the car. I've been thinking about that. Fuel's good for a two-thousand kilometer range. There has to be some reason why he knows that he'll get it back."

A change in note from the motor made a period. The car was making height and a new dust cloud was spilling out from the center of the crescent.

Reflexes quicker than the rest, Ann Riley was clamering back up the mound in a useless bid to grab for e skids before it was too high.

Chevron thought bitterly that he had done it again. He ught to have known what Wagener had said to Cassidy. ut then, he *had* known deep down and had not been repared to believe that he would be written off.

There was time to make a sprint start and grab the girl s the car stabilized at twenty meters and began to turn s nose as though scanning the area. That was the answer: had built-in remote control which would override a cal operator. And with that much fancy circuitry there uld be an armament. He yelled in her ear. "Separate. lake for the next crescent. Hide in a shadow."

They went at a weaving run over a littered moonscape nd the distant operator, restricted to the narrow view of a amera eye in the nosecone, had to pick his target. He hose Chevron and the car lined up for a run-in with a ne beam lancing a thin gulley in the baked earth.

Ann Riley stood still watching it gather speed, halve, en quarter the distance. He was still fifty meters from the imbled wall of the next crescent. There was no chance iat he would make what shelter it had. She screamed, Mark! Behind you!"

She saw him stop and look over his shoulder. The ir's shadow was probing ahead to engulf him. Then it as past and he was lying face down, the car a hundred ieters on, climbing for a turn.

Zakayo had veered off his own course and reached him t the same time. He was lying centimeters from the :ored line. One either side, they lifted his dead weight nd Zakayo settled him over his shoulder in a fireman's t. Then they were pounding on for the rubble line.

The car had banked and was making a wide turn
with nothing in its camera eye but a wheeling panoram
of empty outback.

They got him over the brow and dropped into the cres
cent. Inside, it was better preserved than the first, wit
a complex of circular compounds still standing shoulder
high and one with withered roof beams and a half-mete
strip where the roof of thickly packed clay still kept
shaky hold.

Dust jetted through every crevice as the car made
low run directly overhead and Ann Riley reckoned sh
had traded bisection for the privilege of being burie
alive.

Zakayo had whipped off Chevron's bush shirt an
folded it as a pad under his head. The long, livid sca
across his body was evidence enough in the context.

Ann Riley, kneeling beside the putative cadaver, ha
tears making a track in her dust cake. Partly it was rea
tion after the effort of getting to shelter. Partly it was
kind of overall concern for a situation where sudde
brutatily had become a norm. More as a routine tha
with any optimism she put her ear to his chest.

There was a strong regular beat, on the slow side, b
he was still well at the plus end of the quick-dead scal
It was a surprise at that and she got another. Fine si
hair tickling his skin and the female pollen cloud und
his nose hooked Chevron back into the action.

It was another illustration if one was needed that er
is life. His hands homed on her shoulders and pulled h
off balance. He said, "Paula," with every harmonic
satisfaction and tried to roll her into bed.

Zakayo's gravel voice saying, "Steady, boss. Take
easy," killed the boudoir ambience stone dead and Che
ron sat up. Recall got another boost from the car ma

ng a second run. There was a thin ripping sound under
he wow of the motor as it passed close overhead. A
ection of roof gave a weary sag and bellied in, held up
by a thin web of fibrous stands that refused to part.

Chevron was shaking his head, partly to clear dust out
of his hair and partly to check that it was still on its
stalk. He remembered her warning shout and then total
mobilization of effort for an acrobatic roll. On level
ground it would have brought him back to his feet, but
here had been no time to choose his spot. He had
cracked the back of his head on a clump of ancient
brick.

Ann Riley was saying, "It won't stand any more. If
it does that again the roof will go."

Chevron hauled himself to his feet against the wall with
he mouth of the cave revolving in a slow spin. When he
was standing, feet astride for positive balance, movement
steadied and he said thickly, "It isn't going to make a lot
of difference. Now or later that bastard has stacked the
deck. As I remember the chart, there isn't a settlement
within four hundred kilometers."

Outside there was silence. Creaks from the sagging
timbers were the only sounds on the set.

Ann Riley said nervously, "What's he doing? Why
doesn't he try again and finish it?"

Chevron thought, *It's me he's after. She should have
a chance. Maybe Zakayo can get her back. Now I know
what Wagener was saying to Cassidy. It stinks. It stinks
that Wagener, who knows me well enough, should give
the order, and it stinks that Cassidy should carry it out.
God help me, I've believed in the system and I've obeyed
orders that were against reason. But not again. When
you get down to it, the only loyalty that's worth a clipped
penny is to a person. Experience notwithstanding. Paula*

notwithstanding. If he gets to me the heat will be off. Even a blinkered agent will not go on looking for what he has already found.

Aloud he said harshly, "Stay where you are. Travel at night and rest up during the day. Keep heading due south and you can't miss fertile country."

Then he heaved himself off his wall, picked his polaroid visor from the deck beside his shirt and walked straight out into heat and light that fell on his skin like a tangible weight.

Ann Riley had started after him saying, "No. Don't do it," with a flash of intuition that gave her a précis of the argument that had gone on in his head. But Zakayo's massive arm made a barrier. He said simply, "Don't stop him. He knows what he has to do."

Chevron was twenty meters off walking steadily. They saw him stop and turn slowly, looking every way. Then he was climbing the rubble mound at the end of the crescent and cut off by the horizon of the low lintel.

Ann Riley counted to ten and could bear it no longer. Learning fast in the workshop of the violent life, she stopped straining against Zakayo's arm as though she had accepted the situation and felt his hold go slack. Then she kicked back at his shins and broke free. She was out of the trap like any greyhound and five meters into the open before he could move.

Chevron was standing on his mound looking south, a puzzled man. From the base looking up he was an apocalyptic figure, massive and scarred, set against a brilliant blue backdrop. He said, "I told you to stay put. This isn't your fight. A bit of departmental tidying up."

Zakayo pounding into the circle glistening with sweat said, "I couldn't hold her. I guess she's got her own ideas."

Chevron leaned down and drew her to his plinth. "That's as it should be. There's a shortage of people willing to do their own thing. Mind you, Cassidy has me thinking. He could have finished it. When I came out, the car was over there, hovering and doing a scan. He saw me all right. It stopped and had a good look. I reckon he changed his mind. He didn't like Wagener's brief and he left me with an outside chance. It turned for home and headed off."

Ann Riley had left her visor in the hut and he tipped back his own to see her in natural color.

Hair was sticking in damp patches to her agreeable skull; eyes, with pupils contracted to ration the intake, were dark, luminous disks. Her mouth was half open with effort and deep breathing was giving dramatic tension to the thin fabric of her white shirt.

It was incredible, but it was true. She had meant to join him in a move for human solidarity against the system. That and Cassidy's change of heart were enough to build optimism on.

It needed some toehold. The terrain was all working the other way. There was nothing but distance and heat to cauterize the human will on its stem. Cassidy had not chanced his arm too far. Without equipment or food or water the future was brief, finite and contained.

Zakayo, seeing that she had made her point and saving his breath for the long haul, veered off and picked out the windbreak and the ration pack. He chose another ruined circle and set up the dodger as an awning, then sat under it, waiting for revelation.

Chevron was still looking hard at the girl as though seeing her for the first time. But another fact was niggling for attention. Fine grit was whipping out of the crevices of the old *caravanserai* and stinging his bare

back. He saw her expression change and wheeled round
to see what she was looking at.

Out beyond the earthworks the whole desert was in
movement. A wind had started up as if someone had
thrown a switch. Maybe Cassidy had seen it from the
greater height of the viewing eye in the car.

A dark pall was rolling in and broke over the farthest
crescent as they watched.

When they flung themselves under the awning beside
the *guru*, the sun had gone out and left a stifling twilight,
with fine sand streaming through every crack and noise
beating up to a frenetic crescendo.

VII

RAQUEL CUNLIFFE was disgusted with the weather and was saying so to each arriving guest. After hearing the tape twice, Stafford moved off with his drink. Sucker as he was for the plummy Cunliffe contralto and its enthusiastic emphasis of every key word, he reckoned he had got the message. He pushed out onto the loggia and did a survey for himself.

It was bleak. A cold wind sidled up his metal cloth tabard and rustled his ivy leaves. There had never been anything like it in living memory. The far side of the valley was hidden in driving rain and in the occasional flurry, when the curtain cleared, there was the unmistakable white pallor of snow sticking to the higher ground.

As a name-day gesture, his hostess took her guests to the Pant-y-Bint roadhouse, overlooking the Horseshoe Pass, where there was traditional cooking to remind the sophisticates how their ancestors had to rub along with real bones in their meat. It had always gone down well, a little midsummer madness to act as therapy for the overrational life. But this year it was way out.

Even the pike, seethed in an earthen pot with dates and butter, standing on a dish with an orange in its mouth, could not compete as a talking point with the outrageous season itself.

Stafford went back inside and circulated. All the tales being told were of personal dangers passed, cars navigating blind for the roadhouse beacon, drifts a meter high blocking the farming commune gates, sheep's eyes glaring balefully out of the murk.

One and all, they were amazed at their superhuman

courage in making the trip. In its own way, it would be a memorable party. After their personal experiences, some were ready to judge it would be their last. If four horse-men had galloped up to the mock Tudor door and beaten at it with their whips, there would have been few to question it.

Down on the Cheshire plain it was not good, but up here there was a new force in the newscast accounts of the unprecedented weather patterns.

It was some time before he could isolate the girl in an ingle for a social bite at her neat ear. Food and wine had worked their spell and after its dodgy start, the party was going like a bomb, stoked along by the underlying hys-teria of those under siege.

Only Raquel had a reservation. She said, "Don't do that. I can't *think* when you do that."

"That's the idea. That's precisely why you have gor-geous ears."

He moved his ground to the side of her neck in purposeful progression and had worked along to the fine electrum chain which was the key support unit for her oblong link shift, when she spoke again, full of regret, but firm with it.

"Stop it, Andy. This is *important.*"

Justifiably puzzled he said, "But you usually say that makes you quiver right down to your coccyx."

"So I do, but everything has its *season.*"

"What more appropriate season for a bit of coccyx quivering than your birthday? A simple tribute to the fertilizing of your primal egg. The probability law hit a jackpot."

"Be *quiet*. I have to *think.*"

To help the holographic web on its tangled way, she

took another drink, shuddered delicately, said, "I don't think I *like* that," and slipped expertly out of his hold.

It was true. She had a problem. Stafford moved to a settle and patted the seat next to him. "Okay. Sit down and tell all. If you can sit in that without making little oblong dents in your alabaster can."

"*Seriously.*"

"Okay. Seriously. I'll put my hands on the table."

He did so, with his right thumb standing eloquently out of the heap as though scanning the set.

"Put your thumb down. It *distracts* me."

He did it slowly as though it had independent life and was reluctant.

"It's about Wagener."

"What about Wagener? I haven't seen him. Hasn't he come?"

"No. He didn't seem to remember anything about it."

"Well, you can't be everybody's lodestar. Be satisfied with me."

"It's not that. It's just that I've noticed him more lately. I can't *define* it, but he's changed."

"Nobody else has noticed it. He's still a hardcase, solitary bastard who knows what he's doing. He's taken a lot more individual control work with the outfield. Working too hard I'll grant, but there's nothing wrong with that. What kind of change?"

"It's a *character* change. To me, he's like a different *person.*"

"If that was true the monitor gear would pick it up. You know he gets a physiometric check like everybody else."

"What I'm thinking about would need a *psychometric* check."

"Well, that's not on. Somebody'd have to show *prima facie* cause that he was a security risk. Who'd make a charge like that stick?"

"I might try."

"You'd be out of the section with an 'unreliable' tag before you got to first base. Still it's no bad idea. Then you could take out a pairing contract with me and concentrate on your other qualifications."

There was no answer. She stood up with a musical rattle, heaved a log from a scuttle onto the open hearth, stretched her arms to the mantelpiece and leaned there looking into the flame. Bathed in shifting firelight, her face was unusually tense. True or false, it was important to her.

Stafford said, "I don't pretend to understand it, but if it makes you any happier, I'll see what I can do. I'll watch him like any beaver. It's true enough that stability rates high on the profile. Any change could be dangerous. If he's ill he could show bad judgement. Records keep a copy of every monitor scan for twelve months. I know a man in that section. I'll check the last week. It can't be enough to make a case or there'd already be one. But it might give a lead. Prove you wrong for one thing."

"I'm not *wrong*."

"Who would have thought such an obstinate mule lurked inside that velvet carapace."

Immune to flattery, she went off on another tack. "Do you know Mark Chevron?"

"He was through a month or two back after a rehabilitation bit. Nearly bought it. Some lush Southern had him in thrall. Wagener gave him conditional clearance. Showed his judgment there. Chevron's a good man. Fantastic record. But if he'd gone by the book, Wagener would have shoved him out of the service."

"So he's changed his mind."

"How do you know that?"

"The duplicate location board in Wagener's office. I noticed it today, I don't know why, but his board looked different from the one in operations and I just *stared* at it. When I got outside I could still see it like an eidetic image and there it was."

Stafford said patiently, "There *what* was, for God's sake?"

"Chevron's name tag. It was *striped*. Wagener had put up a *black on red*. He's put Chevron on outlaw status. Maybe he's already put a call out to have him *killed*. That's a change of mind, isn't it? How do you square that with your view that Wagener hasn't changed?"

With Schopenhauer, Stafford recognized that the female mind was incapable of logic. He did his best, albeit bemused by the hank of corn yellow hair and all the curves in the composition. "Changing your mind doesn't mean you've changed your character. We don't know what evidence he had. That's his responsibility and nobody in their right mind would want any part of it. But it has to be done. Somebody has to be in charge and take the hard decision. I don't like it, but it doesn't prove a thing."

"You wouldn't like it if you were *Chevron*."

"If I were Chevron I wouldn't be standing here talking to a mentally deficient sexpot."

"Well, you can go and join him if you like."

Stafford, using useful unarmed combat techniques, twisted her from her hold on the chimney breast and backed her against a supporting beam. She was warm from the fire and finally defeated by circumstance. Her arms adjusted automatically round his neck and anxious

115

thought was momentarily drowned out. A familiar quiver rattled every disk in her spinal cord.

Stafford said, "That's better. I was beginning to think you'd had a personality change yourself."

"I still wish we could do something about Chevron. I hope he's all right."

Separated by some thousands of kilometers from his well-wisher, Chevron was debating whether there was any point in going on. Heat was fractionally less than it had been and the change had wakened him. He was lying on his side under the narrow shelter of the windbreak with his right arm over the girl.

The dark bulk of Zakayo hemmed her in on the far side. Recall flooded in. It was the evening of the second day. Time to strike camp and push on as if there were a purpose in doing so, as if any one of them could make another march.

He should kick them out of the sack, but there was no point in doing it. Give them more time in oblivion. It had been difficult enough to sleep in the stupefying heat. Without the canopy they would already be dead.

Chevron tried to think cool. He imagined a river of ice, snow in drifts, ice again in handy blocks that he could build round himself in an isolating cone. It was no good. He was feverish and light-headed with heat. His tongue was stuck to the roof of his mouth and felt too big for its hole. He was more tired than he ever remembered—dull, stupid, bone-tired with an ache in every cubic centimeter of his mass.

He moved his arm slowly, driving himself first to his knees and then to his feet. Creaseless and indestructible fabrics had come out of it well. Except for a haggard, unshaven face and the sag of his shoulders, there was no

visible record of the last forty-eight hours. Their desic-
cated bones would be found well-dressed.

Once under way, the day's decline was spectacularly
fast. When the first star appeared palely on the horizon,
Chevron woke Ann Riley. He was sorry to have to do
it. There was nothing to offer except grief.

She was too thirsty to speak and stared at him as
knowledge of where she was gathered behind her eyes.

Chevron left her to sort it out and woke Zakayo,
taking care to keep at arm's length. The African had his
knife out of his sleeve before his eyes were fully open.
As time went on, it might get more tricky to convince him
that moving was for the ultimate good. The set smile was
a mere rictus; eyes searching for the man who had win-
kled him out of his comfort were totally without humor.

He said thickly, "Oh. It's you, Boss," with the reservation that he would overlook it this time, but could make
no promises for the future.

He was more cheerful when Chevron broke out the
ration pack, and offered his knife for meticulous surgery.

Chevron was working on a six-day plan. Though he
reckoned·they would be out of program long before that.
There was a half-liter flask of water, a compressed fruit
bar, a chocolate slab and a pack of raisins. On his ration
plan, they had ten grams of chocolate, twice that amount
of fruit bar, eight raisins and twenty-five milliliters of
water each for the day and they took it before they
started the night's march.

Spread out on a tissue, the solids looked ridiculous;
crushed together it would make one reasonable bite.
They ate in silence, making it last.

Silence was internal and external both. Nothing could
be more empty than the desert. Nothing moved. There was
nothing to move.

When they were under way, navigating by the blazing star map, Ann Riley realized she had hit rock bottom in the human situation. All past experience had been burned out.

They were walking three abreast, since there was no road. Looking straight ahead with her companions shut out of peripheral vision, she could imagine she was alone, the original forked animal, conscious of itself, but with no control of its environment.

Walking in step, with the monotonous soft swish of sand under her feet, there was not even any special aural clue that there was anybody else along.

The incredible thing was that the desert had always been there. All her life, insulated by the organization and the artifacts of her century, she had not known of it, except as an abstraction, a colored area on a map. But it had been there, at the back door now and for centuries past, unchanged and unchanging.

It was no wonder the prophets had come out of the desert to wag their bony fingers at the people who lived in cities. If there were any revelation about, this is where it would come. Human pretensions were diminished to a dot. The other world of the sky was more important than the world they lived in. There could well be a brooding genius behind it watching what they were at.

Not a kindly genius though, just a watcher, interested to see how far they would get and at what point they would stop trying. An interesting experiment, like her own on the mice in the cages at her experimental psychology lab.

She stumbled and would have gone headlong into the sand except for Chevron's arm which appeared to come from nowhere.

It could have been a stranger; the croaky voice gave

118

no clues. He said, "Okay. We'll take a spell. Ten minutes. One place is as good as another."

They leaned back-to-back with no word spoken and stood up again when Chevron looked at his time disk and said, "That's it."

He had stopped thinking. He had closed his mind to every issue but one, concentrating all his will on the single task of moving himself and his party in one direction for as long as he could shift one foot in front of another, like a hiberating animal that had retired to a deep center to keep a spark of life burning through a winter season.

He drove them until the sun rose in a yellow glare on their right hand, confirming that they were still moving south and confirming that nothing was changed. They could have been in the same spot as the night before. A light hot breeze had riffled over the sand just before dawn. There was not even a line of footprints to show how they had come.

Raquel Cunliffe was going through the motions on the morning stint at security's coal face, feeling very frail and vulnerable and debating whether or not name-day celebrations were likely to shorten the life span. Without Stafford to consult she was left to her own conclusion and she estimated that every twelve could well lop a year off her ration of time.

When Wagener's summoning bleep sounded in her ear she gave a nervous jump on her high stool. Maybe he had taken to reading her mind at that.

He was sitting foursquare behind his desk, which was not characteristic, and did not even look at her as she crossed his carpet. Consequently, she had no clue on her senstive barometer as to his state of mind.

When he rasped out, "How well do you know Subcontroller Stafford," she was on the wrong psychical foot and looked guilty as hell. However, the time-honored formula came readily to hand.

"We're just good friends."

Wagener lifted his eyes from his desktop. She got a hard look, but it was no transparency maker. Whatever anybody said, there was something different about the man. Although Wagener had never made an overt pass on the sex side, she knew that he had been aware of her as an erotic object and that he knew she knew and that she knew he knew she knew.

The ramifications of that were obscure, given the frail state of her head, and her mouth was half open in a pose that would have looked stupid on a less spectacular face.

Wagener said irritably, "Not socially. Professionally. Do you have any reason to think Stafford would be a security risk? I don't have to tell you that this question and your reply are absolutely confidential."

Raquel closed her mouth and concentrated. Coming after her conversation about the man and Stafford's promise to investigate, it was too pat. It was as though Wagener had decided that the best defense was attack and he would discredit the searcher before he started.

She said slowly, "No, I know of nothing. I would say Subcontroller Stafford was the *last* person to be unreliable. I know he is always cleared A-Okay on the monthly security checks. You must be wrong, director. Why do you ask?"

"What reason would he have to look through the internal monitor files?"

"He is very conscientious. It is in the articles of service that we must be constantly on guard even against other members of the department."

"In other words, you don't know?"

"No. I don't know."

Wagener was suddenly conciliatory and it struck a false note than any yet. "Thank you, Miss Cunliffe. I know I can trust you to be discreet. But as you rightly say we cannot be too careful. You may go."

Andy Stafford coming on duty a half-hour later made a gesture with his eloquent thumb which was to be taken as a sign on a different level from his opening speech. "And how is the fairest flower on the Cheshire plain bearing up today?"

Neither got him far. She said as coldly as her voice would allow, "Nothing on the file, controller. I'm waiting for one-zero-three to call back from Helsinki but it's routine. No problem."

At her console she went through the motions of checking round her section of distant operators. With her left hand she scribbled a brief communique on a quick-erase panel.

He read off: "Watch it. W. knows. What did you find?"

Leaning over, he pressed the cancellation button with his palm and the glowing oblong went clear.

Using the same stylus he wrote, "Unusual surge, but inside tolerance. Proves nothing by itself. Not enough to press for investigation."

He went off to his own desk and Wagener, watching on the monitor, tapped his teeth with the bulky signet ring on his left index finger.

It looked all right. She had said nothing out of the way. He could afford to move slowly against Stafford.

He would have been less easy if he had seen the next message in the series which she switched through so that it came up on Stafford's own memo recorder. "Whatever

you say, I'm *sure*. There's a *change* in him. Who can
we see?"

Change was the one thing which was not coming the
way of the old original in his secluded nook in the medicenter. Wagener himself had wakened suddenly to full
realization of himself as a person and recognized that
it was all bad.

Memory had been recording the score even when un-
derstanding had been blanked out. Now recall flooded in.
Keeping his eyes closed, he tested out one hand at a
time.

No movement was possible. Without opening his eyes,
he tried to shuffle round the mental pictures he had,
to build up the sequence that· had brought him to the
rats' alley he was in.

It was all there, from the slab side of the trash cart
cutting him off from the commuter stream to the last
waking session when a smooth insistent voice had been
asking questions.

Not a doubt but he had answered them in full. He had
used the same techniques himself. Bitter knowledge that
a substitute was holding the top slot in his organization
was enought to turn a mind. But Wagener had not
reached his lonely eminence without a tough insensitive
streak that could take a moral hammering without breaking down into self-destructive guilt. It was another· illustration for the old gag about who is to guard the guardians and he had to check his face to stop it twisting into a
wry grin at the everlasting humor of it.

There was nothing else to laugh at.

He could sense that there was somebody else present
in the room, not too far away either. There was the slight
scuff of movement as the unseen watcher shifted in a

chair and the smell of cigarette smoke as an air current drifted across his face.

It was heavily aromatic, some Turkish element and cigar leaf. Not a common brand. He was still working on the analysis when a hatch slid smartly aside and closed again. A quiet, unemphatic voice asked, "How is he now?"

A chair scraped back and the resident guard moved two steps to consult his gauges. "Blood pressure normal. Heartbeat on the slow side. Still unconscious, but he'll live to talk again if you want that."

Wagener had imagined the guard would be a man; the voice was clipped and precise with no sexy harmonics, but definitely female.

"It's possible. Keep him that way. But Carlos is managing very well. He has settled in with very little trouble. It makes you think, Alva. A plan should be simple but bold. Strike for the unprotected head. In a few days now, we shall be able to withdraw and nothing they can do will protect them from the greatest catastrophe any civilization has ever suffered. And without casualties on our side. It is a stroke of genius."

"I have never understood the details. I am content to do my work."

"Very right. Very proper. But you will have your reward. We shall all do well. When the North is reduced to a few struggling survival units, there will be places for senior administrators. How do you fancy yourself as governor of a province?"

"We have not finished yet."

"True. But nothing can stop us now. I am expecting the signal any day that the polar station has been destroyed. Then we can pull out. There is a ballistic shuttle on standby readiness to take off all personnel from this area."

"What about this one?"

"As soon as I am sure we have no further use for him, you can dispose of him. Put him in a dissecting room. We are not barbarians. We should do all we can to further the interests of medical research. Not that there will be much going on. They will have too much to think about."

Wagener heard footsteps going towards the door and judged that a normal reaction in the woman would be for her to watch her visitor go out.

He opened his eyes a fraction and saw the back of a broad man, partially bald with a thick crescent of dark brown hair touching the collar of his white tunic coat. Insignia on the left epaulette identified him as a senior consultant. That figured. A man of that rank would have free movement anywhere in the medicenter complex. They had got in at the top.

Alva, watching him out, was in the pale blue shirt and white bib of a staff sister with an expensive time disk on the ogee arch of her left breast and a notional hat set like a white marker on a pile of shiny black hair.

She was about thirty-five, with a hard narrow face, and looked as though she would be the bitch of all time to a new batch of probationers.

Wagener closed his eyes again. There was not much to see at that. He felt very tired. With or without anybody in the room, he reckoned there was nothing he could do to get himself off his trundle bed.

A piece of ancient wisdom punched itself unasked out of his much abused computer. A man who has nothing may sleep. Reinforced by the many relaxing drugs still swilling about in his system, the axiom gained total credence. He slept.

If the same proposition had been put to Mark Chevron

he would have clubbed the speaker with any handy rock. Thirst, sand, heat and physical strain combined to make sleep impossible. The yellow glare, hardly diminished by the narrow windbreak, was a continuous silent assault on every raw nerve.

Any movement would disturb the other two. He lay on his back looking at the underside of the canopy through his visor, willing himself to keep still.

Ann Riley's subhuman croak was a relief. She also was awake.

"Mark?"

"What is it?"

"How long before we can move? I can't stand much more."

"Not long. Less than an hour."

"That's long."

He rolled on his side to face her. She was exhausted. Lines of strain tightened her mouth, skin was taut as stretched vellum. It would be a sheer miracle of will power if she lasted another night's march.

She read his analysis and said, "Why wait? Why should we wait? We're losing strength all the time. Why not start now and just go for as long as we can?"

Zakayo sat up. Carrying the most weight, the soft sand had been hardest on him. He seemed to have shrunk inside his bush jacket. "That's sense. There's no advantage in staying here. Let's get on while we still can."

They had a point and Chevron could see what was in their minds. Reaching the target was not on. It had been obvious after the first full day. They might as well stop kidding themselves and go straight on until they had to stop.

The majority could be wrong; nevertheless it was always a powerful force. He said, "If that's the way you want it, that's the way it is."

He opened the ration pack and split the remaining fragments three ways. There was even a drink big enough to swallow. When they were ready to go, he rolled up the windbreak in the full furnace glare. "What about this?"

"Leave it. We shan't need it again." Ann Riley spoke like a cracked Cassandra.

He stuck it in the sand, a marker to show the last rational point reached by the expedition.

For ten minutes, the relief of being free to move outweighed every other factor. There was purpose in it, even a crazy sort of optimism; then the heat began to tell.

Chevron had the securing strap of the windbreak and hooked it to Ann Riley's belt and the back of his own. Then he ploughed ahead, taking her in tow. He closed his mind and set himself to endure, monotonously counting his steps and shoving one foot in front of another as the only activity left to him in a shrinking world.

He was self-hypnotized to move and was a hundred meters along a changed surface before he realized it was so. Instead of undulating sand, they were on a level area like a beach covered with small flat thin stone flakes. It was very hard, with small isolated outcrops of rock.

Ann Riley, unable to shout, waited until he was turned round ready to listen before she said hoarsely, "Zakayo. Wait for Zakayo. He's found something."

The African was ten meters off on his knees and looking at the ground. When he straightened up, they waited for him to rejoin the column.

"*Hamada,* Boss. Stretches for many kilometers."

"So?"

"Much used by wheeled traffic. There are track marks.

They wouldn't last long before they were blown clean. Something went along today."

"We can't catch up with a truck."

"Just so. But they stop to camp. When the light goes they wait for the moon. Or perhaps camp all night and travel by day. That's all right for a vehicle."

"You think we should follow the marks?"

"What have we to lose?"

It was at right angles to the course they were on. But he had a point. Also it was noticeably cooler. The sun was standing on the horizon like a molten penny.

Chevron backtracked to where Zakayo had found a pale golden line against the darker surface of the *hamada*. In its way it was an earnest that they were not the only people left on the face of the earth. It was as good a trail as any other. Without speaking he began to follow it, quickening his pace and with the tether forcing Ann Riley into a heroic shuffle.

He was mesmerized by the line that went straight ahead for the horizon. It glowed for him as light levels fell until it seemed to be splitting his head into two equal parts. He was finally brought to a halt by a dead weight on the strap.

Ann Riley had gone far enough. She was standing feet astride, braced back against the forward pull, head slumped forward on her chest. As he slipped the toggle, she dropped to her knees.

He could only just hear her as she said, "I'm not going on. I'm staying here. I'm staying here."

It was said as much to herself as any other interested party and she lifted her head in surprise when it got a dusty answer.

Chevron's face was a blur, his voice grated with menace.

"Get up."

"No."

To make it even clearer, she went down flat on the deck. Having the strap in his hand brought out the latent Arab slaver. He struck down across her shoulders. Zakayo looming up beside him said, "Steady, Boss."

"Keep out of this."

He tried again.

"Get up."

At the third stroke, she realized that there was to be no peaceful end. Hatred such as no well-adjusted psychologist had ever expected to feel needled her to her feet.

She said, "You bastard. You sadistic bastard," and tried to hit him.

Her balled fist was some centimeters off target and the followthrough swung her round so that she would have fallen again, but he moved in close and held her. It was a swan song. She was out on her feet.

Chevron lifted her. Fire ran along the site of his long scar, as though the healed tissue would give under the strain. But he hoisted her over his shoulder with her head hanging down his back. He staggered in a slow circle, picked up his line and set off.

Zakayo, shoving his knife back up his sleeve, disappeared ahead.

Time was nothing. Pain was nothing. There was only the faint line in the starlight and the will to endure. He was Everyman carrying his burden, with a grave somewhere ahead to dump it in and follow after. But where was it? Where was the hole in the ground where he could lie down and finally be still?

His eyes were playing false; there was an apricot flare set in the track, a small flare with opening petals like a flower. It was blotted out by huge black shadows springing across the flat plain. Devils serving the fire.

Then his burden was gone, but instead of relief he felt a sense of loss.

A wet cloth touched his face. Water was running against his mouth. There was a metal slab side against his back. His eyes focused briefly. The fire was real. There were four people in the party, three men and a woman. The jerrican that was being held against his mouth had a clear legend in black on white: *Northern Region Archeological Survey.*

Whatever menace there could be in that, he could wait to find out. Like Wagener, he slept.

VIII

LIGHT WAKENED Chevron and for a count of three he believed he was under the windbreak. But the smooth down bulge a meter over his head was plain silver gray.

First judgement was that the sun had bleached all color out of the fabric. Then he recognized he was looking at the underbelly of a desert transporter. A dawn breeze filtering past a massive wheel carried a cooking smell. Aural clues confirmed the signal. Somebody was up and about crisping his sausage on an open hearth.

Chevron rolled over and crawled from the burrow. Across his fire, a small bald man in olive drab shorts with a sweat rag round his neck watched him out. Against all belief, it was a morning like any other and the cook admitted it.

"Morning."

Protocol had its place. Chevron said, "And to you."

"You're a lucky one."

It was obviously going to be a time for truth.

"Where's the girl who was with me?"

"She's inside. In the *zenana*. Don't worry, she's okay. Lois has fixed her up."

"And Zakayo?"

The man gave his skillet an expert shake. "He's okay. But I don't go for him. He tried to stick me with a bloody great kitchen knife. Mind you, to be fair, he wasn't altogether himself at the time and he couldn't make us understand that you were back down the trail with your bundle. Surprised us all, a bloody great African waving a cleaver coming out of the infinite wastes and jabbering away in Swahili."

"It would."

"How come you got stranded then?"

"It's a long story."

"One thing about the desert, there's plenty of time. None of that city rush. Still I guess you'd like to eat first. There's coffee in the can. Sausage and eggs okay? Sunnyside up or is that a dirty word?"

"Chevron. Mark Chevron. Engineer."

"Engineer covers a whole lot. I'm Packer. Chris Packer. Glad to know you. Get yourself a plate out of that box and help yourself. We're bound for Tripoli. Finished what we had to do. There was a report that dune movement had uncovered a Roman site, but the fix must have been all to hell or the sand covered it again. We didn't find it. Couldn't have been Roman anyway, they never penetrated this far south."

"How long to get back?"

"It's good travel along this *hamada*. Later on it crosses a regular highway, then we turn off. Not long. Two days maybe. That old cow can fairly shift along. Why should you worry—you were all set for the big sleep?"

The question hung about unanswered. But the group got a hundred percent boost by two fresh arrivals who ducked out of an awning at the rear of the truck.

Packer replayed his greeting tape. "Morning, doctor. Morning, Goldy. This one is back on his feet. Must be solid rubber. Name's Chevron. Chevron, meet Dr. McAskill, the top hand in the enterprise, and Hans Goldmann. Hans is the mechanic. Or engineer if you like. I do a bit of everything. Specialist on carbon dating."

McAskill was tall and thin with short-cropped graying hair like a tight skullcap and round steel-rimmed glasses. Goldmann was medium height, well-built. Light brown hair and beard, eyes very cold and pale blue against his tan. He had already buckled on a belt with a holster and a fancy-handled blaster ready for use. Besides being an engineer he was clearly the armed escort for the academics. He nodded, reserving his comment, and began to assemble his breakfast.

Concentrating on McAskill, Chevron said, "I have to thank you for taking us in. I hear you're going north. I'd be glad to go along until we can pick up some transport."

McAskill's voice was a high-pitched job with a quick and nervy delivery. To fill out the time so that he held the air for as long as anybody else he went in for a lot of repetition. Mobile eyebrows shifted about as though they were a loose feature, running through the nine significant levels of eyebrow position and back to square one.

"Surely, Mr. Chevron, surely. It isn't every day that we snatch three victims from the desert. Not every day by any means. How did you come to be in that state? I say, how did you come to be in that predicament?"

"Equipment failure. We left the car to look at some ruins and a sandstorm blew up. Must have shifted the controls. It took off over the horizon and left us stranded."

Goldmann stopped mopping his plate with a bread wedge and looked hard at the speaker. Packer took another sausage. McAskill said, "Most unusual. Most unusual. You should remember the Arab proverb—trust in God, but tie your camel. Not that there would be anything much in this country to tie a camel to. But there you have it—trust in God, but tie your camel."

"I'll remember."

"I have made no report yet that we picked you up. No report yet. We should do that. As soon as you like we can do that."

"There's no need. We were on a roving mission. No-body expects us back for some days. I'd rather leave it and make new arrangements at the first center with a hire-car service."

"As you wish. As you like, of course, Mr. Chevron. We'll make a move as soon as your companions are ready. What sort of ruins were you looking at? I say, what sort of ruins were they?"

"Not in your line. Baked brick circles and crescents. Used as a night stop for camel trains, I would say."

Lighting a stubby briar pipe, Packer said, "A battered *caravanserai*."

Goldmann flicked a reject into the fire where it spat briefly into blue flame.

Conversation died the death and Chevron stood up. He was about to say that he would take a look at Zakayo, but he was saved the trouble.

The remainder of the group arrived at the same time, Ann Riley and Lois from the hatch, Zakayo from under the blunt bow of the truck.

Lois Taylor, all legs and buck teeth with sandy hair drawn in a severe knot at the back of her head, fixed Chevron with an accusing eye. She was not even side-tracked by Packer's courteous, "Morning, Lois." She said, "This girl was in a terrible state. Her back's *crisscrossed* with blue bruises. I'd say she'd been *whipped*."

It was a brand-new slant on the purposes of the expedition and every eye tracked round to the slaver.

Ann Riley, in white shorts and a red T-shirt with the letters N.R.A.S. in upper case palace script across her chest, put in a good word. "It's all right. Really. I wanted to lie down and die. He was doing it for the best. It's nothing. I'm fine."

McAskill said nervously, "Just so. Just so. Cruel to be

kind. Sometimes we have to be driven to make an effort for our own good. Yes. I can see that. Well, get something to eat and we'll make a start. As soon as we're packed up, we'll make a start."

Goldmann followed Chevron out of the social ring and came up with him on the far side of the truck. Breaking silence for the first time in the new day, he was revealed as a direct gravel-voiced speaker who liked everything clear. "Listen, buster. You might fool the eggheads, but you don't fool me. Don't try anything. I don't believe all that cock and I don't trust you. I'll be watching."

He tapped the grip of his fancy blaster. "This isn't for show. I'll use it. See that rock?" He pointed to a round knob that stood ten meters off. The blaster appeared as if by a conjuring trick in his left hand. A fine, eye-aching beam flicked out in a thread joining it to his hand and the rock split down its center.

Chevron said mildly, "Well done. You're good at that. I'll bear it in mind."

Packer was right about the truck. For its bulk it was spectacularly fast, and Goldmann drove it with the rev counter nudging its red quadrant. Except for a random scatter of small outcrops, the *hamada* was flat as an *Autobahn*. Before the midday halt, they had three hundred kilometers on the clock. Half an hour after the restart they met a two-lane highway crossing at right angles and raised above the desert on concrete stilts.

Goldmann slewed the truck and ran in shadow of the highway for three kilometers before they found an access ramp. Then he pushed to his ceiling speed with the motor in a whine of effort.

Inside the air-conditioned cab, it was a steady seventy Celsius. Zakayo and Ann Riley slept on reclining seats.

Chevron sat in the nose on a squab for three with Mc-Askill and the pilot. Packer and Lois Taylor worked at a table amidships, sorting a job lot of shards from a basket.

McAskill leaned forward and thumped a telltale on the console. "Very odd, that. I say it's very odd. Hardly above eighty outside. Just over eighty. Now I've known it to be one-forty in this area. Must be a fault in the thermal strip. When did you check the heat gauge, Hans?"

Goldmann slowed a fraction to give the dial his attention. It was true. He went back to cruising speed and said flatly, "It's a sealed unit, doc. There's a spare if you want that I should stop and fix it."

"No. No. Don't do that. Look at it when we stop. It doesn't matter. All to the good if it's a bit cooler. I say all to the good if it's cooler."

Packer, with a jigsaw piece poised for identification, said, "There's freak weather all over Europe. Could be that it's worked down this far. There'll be rain next and the desert'll bloom like any rose."

Proving she could do two things at one time, Lois found a jagged remnant that keyed exactly into the one he was holding and said, "I don't understand it. I thought the weather situation was all buttoned up. Don't we have a regulator at the polar station?"

Her companion, hot on the trail of another piece said absently, "True, Lois, true and we pay enough in taxes to keep it there. You remember Orman who used to head our medical team. He went there as director of their medicenter. Doubled his stipend. Wouldn't fancy it myself. Sweet damn all in any direction except snow. Freeze you off at the stalk. He'd be a natural though. Fat as butter. Has a cyber leg too. No frostbite will get at that."

Chevron turned round. Cyber fitments were rare enough in the North. It was a technique that had been perfected in Southern Hem, where indeed there had been a fashionable craze to make it a status symbol. Certain commando units were known to be fitted with one cyber forearm with multipurpose capability.

"How did he come by that?"

"God knows. He had it before he came to us. Very clever with it. All sorts of gadgetry built in. I reckon he could talk to it and get a civil answer."

Outside the terrain was showing a change. The road had dropped to ground level and was running on rock into the foothills of a low range. Eroded rock pillars, showing colored bands of strata like textbook illustrations, shoved out of the litter of scree.

The illuminated dot on the navigator advanced a centimeter. At the next leap it would put them just inside the Northern Region bounday within a few kilometers of Ghat.

McAskill said, "A good passage. I say, a good passage. We will camp outside Ghat. It is not a town of any character. Ghat has no character. But you would find a communications center and even a hire company, if you want that. But feel free to come along with us of course. I say you can stay with us as far as Tripoli if that is more convenient."

A feed road swept purposefully off the highway and led to Ghat. A kilometer from the town it petered out in soft sand and a grove of ragged palms. The town itself was built low with only one tower block rising over its skyline—mainly adobe, broken by clumps of trees and shrubs: a hard-edged composition in green, yellow and white.

McAskill said, "You see, this is typical. It is a non-place. From here it looks attractive. I say, it looks all right from here; but it has not developed. It has had a checkered history. First found in 1855 I believe. Then there was a period of Turkish domination. Then French, then Italian. No character of its own as you will see if you go there. We shall camp outside the suburbs."

Goldmann churned on through the sand, then turned parallel with the outer ring of houses and pulled up in another copse where there was a circular well head and a long thatched shed open at the sides.

Chevron swung himself out and stretched his legs. It was cooler than he expected. The heat gauge told no lie. He called up to the cab. "I'll take a look. Back in about an hour."

He was ten meters off, glad to be moving after the long session in the truck, when the white slave joined him, showing a good turn of speed.

"I'd like to come along."

"Are you okay?"

"Fully recovered. Also I'd appreciate it. I don't like the way Goldmann looks at me."

"He's your pal. Wants to protect you from your sadistic captors."

"I don't know about that. I would say he has something else on his mind."

"We'll get you a *yashmak* in the bazaar."

"It doesn't look as though there'll be one."

Seen close, Ghat had a seedy, run-down look. It was a shanty town. A ground plan of wide throughways and zonal interconnectors had been laid out, but the building lots had not been developed on the scale intended. It was featureless, without a real center except the one tower block which seemed to be the only part of the city plan which had been realized.

137

After twenty minutes of hard walking, they were under its dilapidated porch and looking at an information board, much altered and erased, which listed all the offices in the block. Floor eight had a new tab and a handwritten entry: *Sahara Transport A Vickers, Prop.*

In the lobby, there was a kiosk with a Moorish grille and a brass monkey holding a card in its paws. Chevron read off, "Back in half an hour."

He patted its shiny head and said, "If it goes any colder you'll have to watch out."

On the far wall was an elevator trunk with two cages and another card hung across to do for both. Ann Riley said, "It's like a game where you have clues left about." She went across and read the small print. "No joy, Mark. It says that it's out of order."

They went up the staircase, pausing at every landing to look out at the town. Height did nothing for it. One sector, ragged as a termite hill, could be the ancient nucleus unchanged. At the third floor Chevron stopped and looked again. There were not many people about, and those moving in the square were mainly Arabs with a scatter of Italians, all slow, as though in a somnambulist sequence. But there was one who stood out, a small fat type bustling along with a purpose. There was something familiar about him.

It was not until he was hidden by the overhang of the porch that Chevron's computer punched out the identification. It was Jack Beukes and no other. What he could find to audit in Ghat was beyond imagination.

Chevron tried to remember the list of companies in the porch. There was a chemical firm—Bilma Salt Inc or some such; a multipurpose government office; entrepreneurs of all kinds; a public health center. That was on the floor above the one they were aiming for.

He put his ear to the dusty tile floor. Light, rapid foot-steps were coming up. Miming for silence, he took Ann Riley's arm and hurried her to the next flight.

Beukes was still coming on with the pace of a man who has a long way to go.

At the sixth it was the same. Chevron suddenly knew for a truth that the man was bound for floor eight, the medi-center. Illumination, lighting up other dark corners of his head, gave another bonus. The network of medicenters throughout the hemisphere was a natural for infiltration.

The more he looked at it, the surer he was that he had stumbled on a plain fact. The medical service had its own internal communication system. Its personnel had freedom of access to every site. It had status. No one questioned a medic, wherever he might be. Once you had the idea, you could conjure with it. Here was a state within the state and so much in the public eye that it was never questioned; here was a variant of the old game of hide the thimble in full view on a prominent knob, where everybody saw it and nobody found it.

At floor seven, he led off the landing to a square recep-tion area with doors and corridors leading off from every side. Tired settles were dotted about; an ornate spittoon; two potted palms in regular use as ashtrays; and some crumpled cartons on the deck. It was evidence that life of a kind stirred in the heap. But two clients shrouded in unisex burnooses took no interest and looked as though they might have died some time back.

Chevron said rapidly, "Ann, I want you to do some-thing. Find Sahara Transport and chat up A. Vickers Prop. See what he has to offer. Settle for any kind of car that could take us across the Med. There's a man coming along I want to talk to. I shan't be long. Okay?"

"I'd rather stay with you."

He thought it would have been a fine thing if he had kept the windbreak tether handy and wondered how the two cadavers would have reacted to a little flogging sequence.

Proving that a man can say yes or no, he said, "No, do as I say. I'll be with you before you can say *mamihlapinatapai*."

"Why would I want to say that?"

"Christ knows. Go on. Get on with it."

She went reluctantly, skirting the two sitting figures who made no stir in their wrappers.

Chevron stood close to the door. Beukes' quick tread leveled off at the landing, stopping abruptly, and Chevron believed his theory was to be proved wrong. But it was only the human factor. A quick look through a round port in the hatch showed him the back of Beukes' head. Not built for stairwork, the ubiquitous auditor was wiping his face with a yellow handkerchief.

When he was through, he folded the cloth with finicky regard and cracked off with fresh vigor for the last stint.

Chevron eased back the door and followed after, stopping in the angle until he heard the door to the landing above fall wheezily to its state of rest.

The reception area was standard, except that one palm had given up the fight and withered in its pot. Beukes had taken a sharp right-hand turn and was ten meters off down a white tiled corridor. With hardly a check, he whipped through a door like a gopher disappearing in its hole and the set was empty.

Chevron dug inside the waistband of his pants and transferred his blaster to an outside pocket. The door was a boost to his theory. Faded script said *District*.

Medical Officer. Underneath, a name had been erased and a new one added below it, as though the holder of the office had changed not too long ago.

The new one was *Dr. Zara Chester.* The old one was *Dr. Franz Orman.*

Chevron backtracked to the stairhead and went down two at a time. First things first. It was only prudent, if that still mattered, to secure the line of withdrawal. He found Ann Riley closeted with A. Vickers who had courteously blown the dust off a brochure and was leaning over the back of her chair to help turn the pages. He was a small dark man of indeterminate ethnic stock and looked disappointed to see Chevron.

But business was business. He hopped back behind his desk and bared a full set of very white choppers in a rictus of welcome. "Thees ees your husband, no? I am sure you can satisfy heem. All fine cars. Go wheez, boom, get there in the tweenkling. Very cheap. Also they are thee only ones in Ghat. No other hire company here, only Sahara Transport."

He beamed again, a man on the best commercial pitch.

Chevron said, "How soon can you have one at the porch?"

"One hour." He held up an expressive finger."

"Make it half an hour and we'll take this one—*The Shooting Star.*"

"Regret *The Shooting Star* not available. But eets very brother weell be ready een thirty meenutes."

"Have the documents ready and we'll meet you downstairs."

Outside, Chevron hurried the girl along.

"What's the big rush?"

"Being a clever little psychologist, you'd know about probe techniques, wouldn't you? Getting at the truth in interrogation?"

"I've seen it done with disturbed patients. That's clinical stuff, trying to get at the real worries that lie behind the smokescreen they put up. But its not my field. Why the sudden interest?"

"Keep thinking about it. You might be needed. Nobody can ever tell when a mind bender might be useful. Everybody should have one on any lengthy mission."

The upper corridor was unchanged. Chevron wondered briefly whether he had even seen Beukes in it. The sequence was beginning to seem unreal. There was not much gain either when he pushed open the medical officer's door and ushered Ann Riley into a square anteroom with three other doors opening off and a low crush barrier to keep visitors in their pen.

An Arab girl in a short white tunic paused with an elegant finger marking her place in a filing system and watched them through wide, kohl-rimmed eyes like any gazelle startled at its pool. Three visitors were obviously crisis pressure on the organization.

"What do you want?" It was a frail birdlike cry of despair.

"Dr. Chester. I shan't keep her long."

"Dr. Chester is busy. She has a visitor."

"I know that. I want to see them both. Just run along and say I have a personal message from Dr. Orman."

"She does not like to be disturbed."

"She won't like it if you don't give her that message. Just try it out and see what a happy smile you win."

She was obviously undecided and reluctant to move her finger. Chevron vaulted the rail and was beside her before she could open her mouth. He gathered a stylus

142

from the desk on the way and poked it in the place she was holding open. Then he took her finger—a cool, smooth artifact—and drew it out. "There you are. Easy. You're free as a bird. Go and get your reward."

She looked at her finger as tough to check that it was still okay, but moved obediently to a left-hand door, tapped and went through.

Voices, heard as the door opened, cut off abruptly. A gravel rasp that had no feminine harmonics in it said, "Let them come in."

Dr. Zara's inner room was bigger than the office, with three floor-to-ceiling windows screened by venetian blinds and a whole spread of refined hardware lined along the facing wall. Jack Beukes was sitting on a swivel-mounted chair with its own console on a shelflike arm and a series of open clips which could hold a patient steady for minor surgery or whatever. Across a broad desk, the good doctor was only visible from the waist up and no rational man would want to see any more. She was rectangular in front and side elevation, body and head both. Iron-gray hair fell to earlobe level like so much steel wool.

Beukes made no attempt to claim a long-standing friendship. If he had been rocking in his fancy chair had he since stopped dead, and stared as though he had stubbed his checking pencil on a self-canceling error.

As the clerk closed the door, clearly glad to be out of it, Chevron produced his blaster and said coldly, "Get your hands in sight, doctor. On the desktop. Jack, move real carefully out of that chair and stand with your friend."

Dr. Chester's face was a squat mask mirroring nil affective tone. She asked, "What do you think you are doing? This is a government department. There is no money, if you have robbery in mind."

Chevron said sententiously, "Who steals your purse steals trash. I have come to rob you of your good name."

"Don't speak in riddles. I have work to do."

Beukes had followed the last instruction to the letter and was making a group with the M.O. He said, "Chevron. What's all the malarky? What are you doing here?"

"Questions, questions. I could ask you the same, Jack. In fact that will make a good starting point to the dialogue. Search around, Ann, and see if you can find any gear that looks like an interrogator. I'd like to have one or both of these monkeys wired for sound. Meanwhile don't either of you twitch."

In so far as her craggy face could mirror any emotion, Dr. Chester was looking very relaxed, and a pinpoint of doubt began to grow and burgeon in Chevron's head. He could be way off course.

As if trying to make conversation with an idiot child, she said, "You spoke of Dr. Orman. What do you know of him? Has he sent you to me for treatment? Tell that girl to be careful. There is very delicate equipment in those lockers."

Ann Riley said, "It's all here. I'm surprised they should have such a layout in an out-of-the-way place like this. There's a deep probe unit probably wired to the dentist's chair. I think I can work it."

Chevron stepped smartly round the desk and separated the home team, prodding Beukes forward with his blaster. "There you are, Jack. Here's your big chance to talk freely. Sit back and we'll all listen."

Angled round so that he could watch the doctor, he shoved Beukes into the chair and locked clips in succession on his forearms and ankles.

Ann Riley was holding a plain steel skullcap with a

144

frill of knurled setting knobs and came up behind him as if for a coronation.

Dr. Chester said, "You are making some very tiresome mistake. I hope you know what you are doing. That apparatus is dangerous in unskilled hands."

Beukes had gone white under his patchy tan and was more silent than he had been for some years past.

Chevron said, "That's not a professional attitude, doctor. You'll worry the patient. You should be building his confidence with little encouraging remarks. Like for instance that I don't give a twopence halfpenny damn whether it's good for him or not. Switch on, Ann. See if he lights up with a pleasing glow."

She was some minutes getting it set, making several trips to the subject who had begun to sweat, tightening the micrometer type adjusters for good contact.

Chevron roamed about the room opening file racks and looking at the miniature tape capsules. It was all highly regular. Doubt took an upward spiral. But there was none in his voice when he answered his busy assistant.

She said, "I think that's okay. Ask him a question and I'll tell you if he answers true or false."

"Fine. Tell me, Jack. What would you be doing here, then?"

"This is a government station. I look at the supply position. Check that it operates within the agreed budget. You know that. You must be out of your mind, Chevron."

"True or false?"

"There was a surge, then it steadied. I'll have to analyze. Several factors here. Now I have it. On the whole, false."

Chevron felt the relief of it. He was on the right track.

If he knew what to ask he could get somewhere. But there was not much to go on. He thought about Poldano.

"Does the name Poldano mean anything to you?"

"Not a thing. Why should it?"

"False."

"Why was he killed?"

Beukes made no answer. It had occurred to him belatedly that silence was the better part.

Chevron said, "Can you make him answer?"

"I don't think so. If I reverse the current it might kill him."

"Show me. I'll do that. You take this blaster and watch the medic."

Beukes could not move his head, but his eyes watched anxiously. As Chevron put his hand on the rheostat, he said thickly, "Wait. I understand that Dr. Poldano was engaged in espionage. In that trade a man is liable to accident."

"That's better, Jack. Now you're beginning to think. Since you know so much you must be in the same game. Not on the same side. That gives two possibilities: independent, for the sale of information; or Southern Hem. Which now?"

As he said it, he advanced the wheel by a generous twist.

Beukes gasped and strained against his straps. Chevron killed the power and asked again, "Which now?"

"Southern Hemisphere Intelligence." It was hardly audible.

"What's all the brouhaha? What's going on?" Slowly this time, he began to move the wheel.

Beukes said, "Operation Umanaq," and then sagged down against the holding clips.

At the same time Ann Riley called urgently, "Mark. The doctor."

Busy at his console Chevron had not looked at her for a good half-minute. There had been time for her to move her hands casually from the tabletop and come up with a palm-sized laser with a slender sighting barrel. Beukes had a bodkin hole between his eyes.

It was tracking round to do the same for him, when Ann Riley fired point-blank into the squat nape of the Chester neck.

She fell over the desk, arms outstretched, a sheer hulk.

Ann Riley said, "Oh God. I killed her."

"And very right and proper too. She would have killed me and you wouldn't have liked that, would you? Don't answer that. But that settles it. No more to do here. We'll pick up the transport and get out."

In the outer office he spoke to the girl who was sitting at her desk, buffing her nails and clearly waiting for the signal to head for home.

"Dr. Chester says you are to go. She'll lock the safe and put the cat out. Meanwhile she wants to continue the dialogue undisturbed. Okay?"

A sling purse was ready by the chair. She beat them to the door and then held back as though remembering that guests had their rights.

But Chevron said courteously, "After you, after you. We are merely tourists, but *you* have been working those delicate fingers to the bone."

A. Vickers was on the step in person to hand over his car. It had been new once like the picture in his book; but now it rested at an angle on a roughly welded skid and had a scatter of seal patches on its plexiglass dome.

But the motor delivered a sweet power surge when

Chevron ran over the console and the fuel gauge was registering one hundred percent full charge.

Vickers, flashing his teeth from the pad, called up, "Leave eet anywhere een the Region. Then I weell beell you for collection. Good luck, Mr. Chevron."

As the car rose to its cruising height, Ann Riley said, "We'll need all the luck we can get. What happens when the local police find your friend Beukes and their M.O.?"

Chevron said, "I think I can fix that. Take the stick, I have a call to make."

He fished out his communicator and flipped open the cover, pressed the off-schedule emergency stud and counted five. Then he spoke into the transmitter. "Chevron. Get me to Wagener. But quick."

Raquel Cunliffe said, "Certainly, Mr. Chevron. He'll be glad to hear from you."

At the same time she flashed an urgent appeal to Stafford who joined her at her console.

Chevron heard Wagener answer and said, "Chevron. You'd like to know Beukes on the Government Audit Circuit and Chester the M.O. at Ghat were Southern agents. They're both dead. I'll need you to stall the local security boys, who'll be on my tail in about twelve hours. There's a hookup with the Polar Experimental Station, where the name is Orman. Dr. Franz Orman. The exercise is Operation Umanaq. Don't start balling out Cassidy, he rid his best. What instructions do you have for me?"

"Where are you?"

"Ghat."

"Stay there. Call in every six hours. There'll be something for you. Does Cassidy know of this?"

"Nobody knows except me."

"Good, keep it that way. Out."

Raquel Cunliffe cut the link with Wagener and broke in.

"Mr. Chevron."

"Still here."

"Use your own judgment. Check on any instruction you get. Out."

IX

"YOU KNOW what you've done?" Adam Stafford was taking a cool look at his apple. She wriggled nervously on her high seat.

"What then?"

"Just broken about the most serious rule in the book."

"So now we'll *know*. Chevron's on to something big. If Wagener ditches him, he *must* be round the twist. That's all the evidence we need for an inquiry."

"Try to use it and you'll be in the brig before your feet can touch."

"Don't make *difficulties*."

A telltale glowed purple on her console."

"There you *see*. Wagener's going out. That's unusual at this time. I bet he's going to see somebody about it."

Stafford crossed his Rubicon. "Okay. You just could be right. I'll take a look. But I rely on you to bring grapes on visiting days and comfort my mother."

He picked up Wagener's erect figure as it surfaced from the subway, and followed fifty meters off as it moved smartly through reduction bays on the interzonal walkway.

It was not a long ride. Wagener peeled off again at the tower block which housed the Regional Medicenter and hurried across its porch without a backward look.

Stafford reached the lobby in time to see his chief's back cut off by the closing hatch of an elevator cage. He pushed through a mixed crowd round the reception kiosk and read the legend on the panel. The elevator was bound for the twenty-second floor, a private area hatched in green, labeled Government Research Center. Not a doubt but there would be a checkpoint. Wagener would have his chief official's pass, but anybody else would be screened.

A second cage homed beside him and three people came out. Without any precise plan, he whipped in ahead of an elderly man handicapped by a plaster cast on his left leg and stubbed the activator for floor twenty-one. Standing on a rack designed to take a stretcher, he checked out the roof. There was an emergency release hatch and he shot back the clips and lowered it inside. A telescopic ladder on the outer surface dropped to the deck, narrowly missing his head, and he climbed out into dim light and the hiss of fast-moving gear.

Moving delicately, he retracted the ladder and closed the hatch as the cage slowed to a stop. Floor twenty-two was at eye level when he stood upright and Wagener's cage was still at its station.

Handgrabs in a recess on the left-hand wall of the trunk caught his eye and he hung there as his own cage began to go down. Swinging out, he got his toe under the hatch release and eased it up. The double doors opened a centimeter, ready for a cage to complete the circuit and roll them open. Through the gap, he could see the landing, where Wagener was talking to a civil guard with a carbine hung on his shoulder.

Even the Special Branch chief was having some difficulty getting through. Security was tight.

Stafford climbed past the twenty-second and looked round the trunk. Just under the sill a half-meter square grille was secured to the interfloor face by six wing nuts. It could be a ventilation duct. It could get him down the corridor.

He worked round clockwise from top left and had four nuts free when a draught began to fan up his slacks.

The elevator was coming up. Sweat running down his neck he cleared the fifth, loosened the last and swiveled the fitting to hang by its final hold.

Getting in was another matter and the shaft was vibrating gently under his hands when he managed to angle round for a feet-first entry. The side of the fast-moving cage brushed his hair and his open mouth filled with dust.

Edging in and feeling round with his feet he judged that he hit a junction two meters down the hole. He bent himself to go left and worked himself round until he was facedown, then he went forward along a circular conduit with a couple of centimeters free play on either side.

It was not entirely dark. Patches of diffused light showed up where ventilation outlets were set in the roof below. Every five meters there was a wider space where tributaries from left and right made a crossroad.

Head poked over the second ventilator on the main highway, he stopped for a spell looking down into the white tiled corridor. Wagener passed below, stopped a little way ahead and turned off into a room on the right.

Stafford crawled on to the junction and turned right. Five meters along the trunk he found a familiar flattening of the tube and a surface grille.

Familiar also was the face staring up from the cot below. Wagener, with the fastest strip in the annals, had gotten himself into the cot in a sterile shift.

A cold voice with no trace of bedside manner was saying, "You should not have come. You were told to make no direct contact with this place."

Wagener's voice, though the figure on the bed did not move its lips, said, "I have to use my judgement about that. I regard this as an emergency situation. The code name of the operation is known to the agent Chevron and possibly to his associates. It was a great mistake to use a geographical term. It gives a lead."

"But you are in a position to suppress that information. See to it that the man is not picked up alive. I only hope that your ill-considered action in coming here does not have serious consequences. The end however is in sight. In a few more days the process we have started will be irreversible. Do not lose nerve now."

"It is not a question of losing nerve."

"You have passed on the information. I will take what action I think is justified. Meanwhile do what you should have done already."

Stafford began to ease back the way he had come. He did not like leaving the old bastard on his bed of pain, but he didn't fancy his own immediate future either. There was nothing much good in the equation, but there was no doubt he had to get himself to where his information could be processed.

Ann Riley touched down in the sand five meters from the truck and Zakayo ambled over from the barbecue to meet them. When the side shield was wound down he leaned in head and shoulders. "That Goldmann; he's been working on McAskill. I guess he has a suspicious nature. Got him to call through to their headquarters and report that we'd been picked up. It'll be all over the territory on the evening newscasts."

It had been a silent ride. After his call to Wagener, Chevron had been withdrawn in a session of total concentration, reviewing what data he had and trying to make it fall into a coherent pattern. Ann Riley was facing up to what she had done and could not cover it with a shroud of expediency. Maybe it followed the logic of the moment in time when she had pulled the trigger, but it was out of line with the whole run of life's experience up to that point.

Means are as important as ends. By opting for the violent solution, she felt she had unfitted herself for any part in the future, even though it could be proved to her that any kind of future hinged on fighting the enemy at the gate.

Maybe it was a constitutional issue. She was a natural pacifist and Chevron was a natural killer. It was anyway outside the reach of intellectual debate; it was a feeling and she felt miserable.

Even Packer's cheerful greeting at the fire made no difference. He went on at length about the jar he and Lois had assembled, all good professional stuff that would have had a learned society rolling in the aisles. But there was tension elsewhere. McAskill was nervously conscious that he had breached the hospitality laws. Goldmann was coldly watchful.

Finally McAskill broke into Packer's monologue. "Well, Mr. Chevron. Now that you have your own transport, I expect you will want to continue your journey. I say, I expect you will want to go on. We have some surplus stores now that our trip is shorter than we planned. Hans will fix you up with anything you need. Enough for a day or two until you can organize provisions. Where will you be heading for? I say what is your next objective?"

Chevron said, "South. Straight back to Gambia. I have to settle about the car we lost. That's a very civil offer. A day's supplies will be enough. Make out a bill and I'll frank it with my credit serial."

"There's no question of payment. Glad to oblige. I say glad to be able to help. When will you leave?"

"As soon as we can. Say in half an hour. I'll load those stores right away if that's okay, and many thanks."

Goldmann looked reluctant but moved off slowly to the sand truck. It was clear that he thought they ought to be held until some answer came to McAskill's signal.

In twenty minutes the transfer was made and they gathered again round the fire in the short twilight, with Goldmann trailing two steps behind Chevron.

Packer had carried a portable actualizer out of the truck and sited it under a palm tree. A commerical for stuffed figs had built up in 3-D on the sand. Two cynical camels and a nude holding the product had joined the enclave. It faded on the punch line, "Give Achmet a fig tonight," and was replaced by a news desk and a seated figure in white jacket and red fez.

This one riffled through a sheaf of papers and said, "This newsflash is to tell you of a dual murder in the ancient town of Ghat."

Chevron sidestepped and turned on the ball of his right foot. He caught Goldmann's hand as it closed on the butt of his fancy blaster. For a short count there was a deadlock. Then Goldmann tried to chop flat-handed into the side of Chevron's neck.

Chevron swayed away and the extended fingers brushed the collar of his shirt. Then he had both hands on Goldmann's short-cropped head and was helping it on its downward path.

Off balance, Goldmann sprawled facedown in the sand, recovered in an elastic rebound and was coming up for a second round when Chevron's voice cut coldly through the action. "Don't try it, Hans. Drop your belt."

The blaster lined up on his forehead clinched the

deal. There was no immediate future in it. Zakayo with his knife and teeth catching the firelight picked up the belt and slung it over his shoulder.

Attention round the circle was distracted by the newscaster. He had gotten to the meat of his message. "Last visitors to the medical unit were a man and a woman, strangers in the district. The woman was dark, slim-built, wearing white coveralls. Aged about twenty-five. The man was above average height, powerfully built, wearing a bush shirt with green buttons. Eyes could be gray or green. Light brown hair. They are required for questioning. That's all, folks. We'll keep you posted. Call in if you see these people. North Regional Actualities offer a fifty credit handout for any useful information."

Lois, an impulsive girl, said, "It's them," and put her hand to her mouth to shut the stable door when the horse was gone.

Chevron said, "Don't worry, Lois. I'm not going to snatch your little pot. It's a long story, but isn't the way you think. Believe it or not, but the two who died were enemy agents. In case you get any false ideas about that you'll have to come along. Switch off the actualizer, Chris, and lead the company over to the car."

McAskill said, "I warn you, Chevron, you're making more trouble for yourself. I say you're adding to your problem. My organization will not stand for interference with its officials. I shall put in a complaint at the highest level."

"You can put it where you like, of course—your privilege. Meanwhile get along to the car."

Overloaded, the car was down to fifty percent of its ceiling and Ann Riley at the console could only clear the copse by half a meter. Chevron, sitting cross-legged in the freight bay with his blaster resting on his knee, called down the aisle, "Take it slowly, Ann. Follow the road we came in on. Count off ten kilometers and stop."

She ran the distance in twelve minutes, conscious of the strained silence at her back. When the car planed down to an uneven halt, Chevron said, "Believe me, McAskill, I'm sorry to do this. But more hinges on it than a return for services rendered. I need to be sure that none of your party starts shouting the odds before we get away. Just tumble out and start walking. You can't miss Ghat."

With the car shrouding the castaways in a minor sandstorm, Chevron leaned out and pitched Goldmann's gunbelt into the murk. He shouted, "Don't shoot until you see the whites of their eyes."

Then he was pushing in beside the pilot and weighing up the sparse detail on the illuminated chartspread.

Chevron said, "Everything points to the Polar Scientific Complex. The omega point of the enterprise is somewhere there. Orman moved there. Poldano was boning up on iceflow theories. Umanaq rings a bell somewhere."

Ann Riley said, "It's a location. A mountain, I think. Near the North Pole. It's mentioned in polar exploration. It's an Eskimo word."

"Now you tell me. How long have you been sitting on that mine of information?"

"I thought I'd heard it before, but I didn't know where. I let it hang about in my subconscious and it finally came up with what it knew."

"You have a good line in subconsciouses. Remind me to take a look at it when we have a clear day."

Zakayo was drumming with his knife on the back of the squab and brought in a practical note. "That's a long way. This beat-up shuttle isn't going to get us that far."

It was true and it brought up another issue. Chevron said, "Us? Not us. You're in deep enough. Tripoli's not far and it's big enough for you to lie low. I go on from there alone."

The car planed down and Ann Riley made a neat landfall beside the road. She folded her arms and asked reasonably, "Do you say that because you don't think we're as clever as you are? Or because you don't trust us? Or because you don't think we can take it? I didn't start on this expedition as a volunteer. But now I'm in I want to see the end of it. Also it's me the posse is looking for. I killed Chester."

"Nobody knows that."

"I know it and that matters."

Zakao said, "I feel that way. You may be glad of somebody to watch your back. I'd like to go along."

Chevron considered it. He reckoned they had a point. From a practical count, it might make the difference of getting there or not. He realized that he had simply wanted to keep her out of further trouble. Maybe he had no right either on a personal or public basis to stand in the way. He said, "That's a vote of confidence that I appreciate. If that's the way you want it, that's the way it is. Take her up then, Ann, set a course for Tripoli and give her all she's got."

Traveling without lights except for the glow from the navigation spread, the car trailed its moon shadow over the desert. Every hour on the hour the newscasts repeated the account of the episode at Ghat. The intruders, it seemed, had vanished without trace, but regional security forces had been alerted. A car-hire operator had come forward with a story that might help. There was a description of the shuttle. It was unmistakable and arrests were expected at any time.

Chevron said, "The desert is like the sea. It can't be searched in five minutes. We're safe enough until we approach a main center."

"Which is what you've just said we intended to do."

"There's a transcontinental rocket service from Tripoli. We'll take that to Copenhagen. Then it's one hop to Reykjavik. Spitting distance from there."

"Just like that?"

"The finger isn't on Zak yet. He can book the passage. I know a man in Tripoli who can fix us up with documents. Get you a blonde wig for a start. That should look very fetching."

"The gunman's moll bit."

"That's it. Just undulate that neat can a little and wear a fixed smile and who knows what personality change will follow?"

After a long detour to bring them in along the coast from the east, the outlying suburbs showed up as a luminous filigree one hour before first light.

Chevron, lying flat on the deck and looking through an observation panel, conned the car like any lead-casting mariner through a maze of darkened alleys. Finally, he took them down in the parking lot of an all-night bistro with a sky sign in crimson, *The Knot of Heaven*.

He said, "Go inside and see how the other half lives. They won't ask too many questions here. I'll be about an hour. That gives you time to unravel the knot if you find it. See you."

Before Ann Riley could reply, he was out of the hatch and she saw him melt into shadow and disappear.

Chevron went up the crazy outside fireladder of a crumbling apartment house he recognized that the enterprise hinged on a long shot. Two years ago Lavery had lived there and he had not heard anything on the grapevine to say that the agent in Tripoli had been changed or moved. But it was a flexible service. Any one of a hundred contingencies could have operated in the interval. He was not even sure that he could find the room.

Seven floors up, moving like a cat, he left the narrow ladder and worked along a narrow balcony to a fire door. It was locked. A brief searing blast from his handgun melted out the tongue and it opened inwards against all safety regulations.

He was in a dingy corridor with a small courtesy light at the far end, a stairhead and five deeply recessed doors. The number thirty-three rang up on his computer. It was the third of the three opposite the stairs.

Lavery, a Mediterranean type, surfacing from sleep with a weight on his chest said, "Not now, Zulaikha. Go home." Then he tried to reach the laser under his pillow.

Chevron said, "Steady, you lecherous swine. What amazes me is that you've lived so long."

"Chevron. Mark Chevron."

There was a harmonic in the tone that suggested he had heard the name in the more recent past.

"The same. Now take it easy, there's something going on that I don't understand. But you can discount anything Wagener told you for a start."

"You would have to say that."

"Look, I could have killed you. But I need help. You can talk to Wagener later. The way I have it from headquarters, they're not too sure of him."

"So?"

"I'm going to let you get up. Don't do anything rash until you hear me out."

It was early to follow a closely knit argument, but Lavery showed that he was earning his pay by putting in the intelligent question. Finally he said, "It figures. There's a bad smell abroad. I tried to raise Kurt Glasman in Palermo. No dice and no clue where he went. The rats are in and nibbling the fabric. I'll do it. But you surely took a chance. The word has gone out. Don't push your luck on the way."

"I won't need to. Fix those papers but quick and I'll leave you to your erotic fantasies."

"Not fantasies, believe me. This outpost is all go."

"Move it along, will you?"

Lavery was forty-three minutes to the second and Chevron had begun to believe that his eloquence had been wasted. When there was a double tread in the corridor, he reckoned that the *gendarmes* had been called.

He waited behind the door with his blaster poised for the shot. But it was Lavery with an Arab swathed in a baggy shroud with a yellow belt, carrying two smart grips.

Lavery said, "The impossible always take a little time. But it's all set. Boarding cards for the 0800 T.C.R. to Copenhagen. You're a production engineer, the girl is your secretary. You've been visiting a component factory for Paramatic Rotating Tools. Drilling, burring, tapping, nut running, reaming—it's all in the brief—give you a nice line in ambiguous conversation. The African is separate. Trade rep for a food-packing concern. Baggage here for the customs man to turn over, with a packet of dirty pictures to give you a sympathetic image."

"I'll do it for you sometime."

"I hope not. Yusuf will take you to pick up your party and then take you on to the terminal. There's a wig for the frail and an outfit for you. Good hunting. Watch the frostbite in your extremities."

Chevron hesitated and Lavery took it without offense.

"I know. I know. Yusuf could take you to the precinct guardhouse. Do you want me to come along?"

There were so many imponderables that Chevron reckoned he had to take something on trust. "That's all right. So long as he knows that if there's any problem he's the first to go."

Yusuf answered for himself in a voice that had no hint of the orient about it. "Do not worry, Mr. Chevron. I understand. All will be well."

Light was edging over the city as they reached *The Knot of Heaven*. Chevron spent his time in the narrow confines of the cross-city shuttle giving himself the international rig of a transcontinental commuter. There was a hair dye and a skin-tightening cerement that gave minor but subtle refashioning to the overall plan of his face.

Yusuf, having parked the shuttle at the porch, said sincerely, "That is a very good job, Mr. Chevron. I would not buy a rotating tool from you; but it is very credible that you would try to sell me one or indeed several."

Chevron, always having liked the line, said, "Keep the motor running, I'll be right out."

Inside, he was a prey to doubt. *The Knot of Heaven* was a maze of hanging multihued gauze. Atonal music channeled everywhichway baffled all sense of direction. It was the Cloud of Unknowing given a location in space.

A nude Nubian with a shaven head of great classical

beauty and breasts like plump tusks materialized as though uncorked from an elegant bottle.

"I'm looking for a European girl with dark hair."

"Noelle? I will see if she is available."

Chevron recognized that it was false to imagine that all the world was thinking what he was thinking. "No. A visitor. With an African."

"Oh. This way. They are in the bar."

At the womblike center of the maze, a small oval clearing was close-packed with voyeurs of every age and shade. An acrobatic stripper was bringing a popular act to a close in a complicated sequence with a lighted cigar. When he tapped her on the shoulder, Ann Riley said, as though not for the first time, "The answer is no. Go away."

She was not altogether sure when she saw him full-face.

Chevron said, "It is I. Your friend of the desert. Straighten your tiara and follow me."

She was silent all the way to the car and listened to his exposition without a word. She weighed the wig in her hand as if debating whether to wear it or not.

"What is it? Don't you want to live your life as a blonde?"

"It's not that. I just wonder whether it's worth the effort. What are we fighting about? What has Northern Hemisphere got that we need to struggle to preserve it?"

"It's got freedom."

"Freedom to kill and visit places like that."

"You're tired. This is the hour of the day for pessimism. Your work in Accra was worth doing. You can choose what you do. Don't be deceived by the froth at the top of the glass."

Zakayo said urgently, "Visitors. Just pulled in by the porch."

A long red civil guard shuttle had sidled to a halt across the entrance. Yusuf was already moving and they were lifting out of the compound as the guards spilled out in a copybook raid maneuver.

Yusuf said, "They are very discreet. They will not say anything. But the sooner you are at the terminal the better."

For Ann Riley, the green and blue spread of Reykjavik with its parallel rows of small white houses was as unreal as a picture card. Movement and a succession of images had been too fast to digest. She knew intellectually that she had shifted her thinking eye over a quadrant of the globe, but it could have happened in a travelogue to somebody else. She had eaten, she had slept fitfully. They had seen the fantastic weather pattern over Europe and the spread of the white shelf which was already sending tongues out beyond Greenland.

Reykjavik was a small oasis, under siege, holding back the white tide that threatened to engulf it by the four tower reactors on its perimeter.

Chevron broke into her closed circuit. "It's all fixed. There's a constant service to the Polar Complex. Freight, personnel changes, everything comes through Reykjavik. No problem. Always spare seats on a transport."

Now it was near, she saw the problem as insoluble. "But what can you *do*? If it was simple it would have been done already. You saw the weather they're having. They must have had a government inquiry to see that the station was doing everything it could."

"That's so and it must have been accepted that it is, but there's something going on there that doesn't add up.

Stay in Reykjavik. I'll book you in at a guest house. You'll be able to read a good book and knit yourself a sweater."

"Having come so far I'll go the whole way."

It was true what the steward said. Except for a check of their papers and a call to the complex itself to notify reception that they were on their way, there was no resistance to the request for passage.

The sun was low and so watery that floodlights were lit all over the landing area when the service shuttle planed down at the Polar Scientific Complex. A massive heart-shaped hump of mountain overshadowed the few surface installations. Lines of pinpoint red light ran into the semidarkness and the shifting spirals of fine snow, giving definition to the run of the underground city built in the permafrost.

It should have been God's gift security-wise. There was only one way in. Maybe it was, at that, there was also only one way out, and the organization might prefer to do its screening on the site without all the publicity that would follow if it appeared to be excluding the public.

The locale was God's gift to a potential suicide. The short walk to the squat terminal block proved that. A man only had to walk out and a few hours later a medical team would be excavating for him with a heat hose.

At the desk, a clerical android scanned the visas issued in Reykjavik and selected the appropriate welcome. "Visitors will be accommodated in block H on level three. Please take a copy of the handbook. Regulations must be followed exactly. This is for your own protection. The information kiosk on level three will tell you how to reach the department you wish to contact. If you have any difficulty, you should call the Town Manager's Office, Extension TC 001 on any internal video. Your heavy baggage will be brought to you."

At level three, in a circular domed lobby, tricked out in pleasing pastel shades to soothe the minds of the long-term trogs, Chevron saw his word for the first time in print alive. Districts on the level were listed with directions and distances. There was a dormitory area for the residents, a recreation zone with a choice of clubs, theaters, a transit hotel, restaurants, and a heated pool. There was also a medicenter with a traditional name. *Umanaq General Hospital.*

He said soberly, "That's it, then. The very heart of the enterprise. A brief stop at the hostel for maintenance and we'll take a look at it. Our boat swims freely in the stream and current of this affair."

In that, he was only zealous in following the regulations listed in the book. It was number one priority in red type. "All visitors registering at the Midnight Sun hotel must present a clearance certificate from the medicenter. The complex is germ free and long-term residents lose immunity. Visitors must be prepared to have inoculations brought up to date."

The designers had given thought to the layout. Vistas of carefully chosen color led the eye out of its confining cage. Translucent areas gave a sense of great space. It was a tribute to human ingenuity in an alien environment. A monorail shuttle took them from the hotel along a half-kilometer of brilliant white tunnel to Umanaq General where the duty clerk, a trim redhead, ushered them into a waiting room and put in a call to bring the duty medico out of his hole.

There was a wait, five minutes by the clock. When they got service, it was from a tall gray-haired type with an incongruously youthful face, wearing slacks under a housecoat and a lapel badge that read **Dr. Fabiola Dent,** looking less than pleased at the break in her living time.

She hurried through into a surgery, closed the door and spoke to her public through an intercom in a harsh rasp. "One at a time. I'll take the woman first."

Ann Riley said, "She's a biomech. I know the type. All hardware under that well-preserved skin. Could be about a hundred."

Whatever the age, she was brisk. Ann Riley was out in three minutes flat, clutching a chit and looking puzzled.

"I showed her my medical card. It's all up to date on every jab that ought to be necessary, but she insisted on a booster. I don't get it."

Zakayo, called next, paused at the door. "I don't like it. What would she do that for?"

"Just leaving no stone unturned. They won't make a move yet. Why should they? They're used to visitors flowing in and out. Don't worry."

"I hope you're right."

When he came out he was still doubtful. "She had the shot all ready in a serum gun. Fancy marksman—just picked it up off of her blotter and aimed over the desk." He rubbed the site in the left shoulder. "Not a thing to feel. She's got a good gadget there. I'll get back to base and wait for you there."

"Do that. You go along with him, Ann. I'll be with you as soon as I finish here."

He expected opposition but she was suddenly docile and followed Zakayo out.

A second irritable transmission from the medico had Chevron moving for the surgery. On the way, he picked up an oblong NO SMOKING plaque from a coffee table and wedged it under his shirt on the left side.

Cold blue eyes faced him across the desk. Seen close,

Fabiola Dent looked inhuman as an android. Emotion had been amputated with her other fallible organs. Zakayo's instinct was dead right.

She said, "We have to be sure here. An epidemic could decimate the staff. That would be serious."

The gun came up almost casually, but the aim was exact. A woman of habit, she had found her preferred spot and stuck to it. Chevron felt the thump on his plate and said mildly, "You don't believe in choice. What is that? I might be allergic."

The eyes gave nothing away. "You elected to come here. You must follow our necessary rules."

"How do I get to see Dr. Orman?"

"Do you know Dr. Orman?"

"I have a message for him from an old acquaintance. Dr. Chester."

Even a biomech could not wholly escape the biological heritage. The Dent eyes blinked involuntarily. But she rallied gamely enough. "Wait in your hotel. I will see that he knows. But I cannot guarantee that he will see you. He is a very busy man."

Chevron took a shower, gave himself a cigarette and padded round his room in a striped towel. A connecting door to Zakayo's neighboring room had been left locked and he pounded on the panel.

"Zak. I'll pick up Ann and see you in the bar in five minutes. Okay?"

There was no answer.

He dressed slowly, appreciating the comfort. It could have been any well-appointed hotel room anywhere. It seemed incongruous to be shoving the blaster in the waistband of his pants. He was out of phase with the sheer ordinariness and stability of the set.

In the corridor he tried Zakayo's door. It was open and he went in. There was no sign of the African, but a shower was hissing quietly in the washroom.

He stood in the open doorway. "Zak?"

Again there was no reply and the dark shadow on the ground glass screen was stock still.

Zakayo had wedged himself so that he could not fall. The haft of his long knife was sticking out of his chest. Water in the well was still running ruby red.

Bitterness choked Chevron's mind. He was the Jonah of all time. He had brought them half across the world as a useless sacrifice. Dr. Fabiola Dent must be shaking her tin guts with Homeric laughter.

And what about Ann Riley? She had no handy knife, but there was no shortage of means for a clever girl.

Chevron sprinted for the end room of the corridor and tried the door. It was locked. He used his blaster to sear out the bolt and burst in.

She was lying facedown on her trundle bed, very still, nude as any needle. Lois was dead right. Her back looked like that of an atrocity victim.

X

STAFFORD FINISHED a well-told tale and looked at the three faces opposite to see how it had gone. Encouraging heavy breathing from his left assured him that it had gone like a bomb with Raquel Cunliffe, but the boiled blue eyes of the Commissioner for Internal Security showed no light of joy.

He drummed on his desk with a knarled thumb and asked, "You are prepared to be interrogated electronically?"

"Yes."

"What you say has very serious implications. It means that infiltration has gone deep. For my part I am inclined to believe you. You realize that it is unlikely that we can save your controller? At the first hint of inquiry, he would be killed and disposed of."

"I was coming to that, commissioner. If he is still held there, it might be possible for a small cutting-out party to get to him. Give me authority to take three of the special staff and I will try. The situation could not be made worse. He will have valuable information if we can get him away alive."

The commissioner said, "Not so fast." He pressed a stud and a guard entered stage left. "Wait outside. We will call you back. Believe me I understand the urgency of the situation, but precipitate action may do more harm than good. Have patience."

They were fifteen minutes by Raquel's earlobe time disk and Stafford was called back alone to her great disgust.

Once committed the commissioner was brief. "Your

account is accepted. Also your interim plan. Before you leave here, guards will have been positioned to seal off the Special Operations unit. Nobody can say at this stage how far the guard detachment at the medicenter is involved in the conspiracy but they are nominally under Western Command authority. A senior staff officer will make a routine inspection visit to coincide with your attempt to reach Wagener. You will have one hour and then the whole research establishment will be given a fine screening. Good luck."

One at a time, at discreet intervals, Stafford's group joined the sick parade in the busy lobby of the medicenter. One had a spinal support and the others courteously gave him first go at the elevator. It was a touching scene and showed that human solidarity was no dead duck.

Once inside, he stripped off and assembled a light machine carbine which was fitted neatly into the package.

Stafford had the roof trap open and was up top with a vibrator hanging on a lanyard round his neck. As the cage hit its check pin on the twenty-first floor, he grabbed for the inset ladder and swung off. Before the others had closed up, he had sliced through the framework of the grille and passed the center piece back to be chocked in any handy niche.

Familiarity shortened the route. He reckoned if he did it every day he would set up an international record. As the last man entered the shaft, he was looking down at Henry Wagener as though he had never left.

Vision was limited. There was no sound from the room below. Wagener had his eyes closed and could be dead or deeply asleep. On the left he could see the shoulder and arm of a seated figure.

Wagener was still wired for sound. It would only take a split second for the attendant to throw a key. It was all going to depend on reaction times.

Methodically he worked round the wing nuts which held the grille. Then he planted his feet on the shoulders of the man behind who gripped them fast and went into a sequence which he had worked over in his head until it was set there like a blueprint etched in acid. Left hand shoved the cover clear. Right hand, head and shoulders plunged down in the gap.

Impressions crowded him. The room was smaller than he guessed. There were two people other than Wagener in it, both very close, a woman by the bed and a man sitting back to the door with a carbine across his knees.

Curiosity worked for him. Before reaching for her console the woman had to look up to see what was happening to her roof.

Mouth open showing a good set of even white teeth, auburn hair falling away from her face, foreshortened, symmetrical, a jewel at the bottom of a well, surprise was caught and went rigid as a red bodkin hole opened between her eyes and Stafford was ranging round for a second target.

The man tried. The carbine was coming up and he had first pressure on its firing stud when the laser on continuous beam flicked its thin bright rope across his neck. He fell forward across Wagener's feet.

It was no surprise to Henry Wagener to see figures materializing out of the woodwork. He sighed and closed his eyes again. Illusion had gone deep. They had finally gotten to his core.

Even when Stafford carefully drew off his skullcap and Foden, the second man, unclipped his wrists, he was no sure that it was a real sequence. Orientation was not helped

172

by the silent mime. But he went along with it. It was a change and any change could be expected to be for the better.

When he was wedged in the trunk with Foden going backwards guiding his head and Stafford shoving from behind he reckoned that it was an elaborate ploy even for an espionage group. It must be happening to him.

Conviction grew with the journey. Swathed in a head bandage, he limped across the lobby to a waiting shuttle. There was even some of the old gravel in his voice when he said, "Right, Stafford. Fill me in. What's been going on in the section?"

At the operations room, Raquel Cunliffe said, "I can't raise Wagener. Sorry controller, that *phoney* Wagener. I know he's in his room, he took a call about two minutes back; but he doesn't answer."

Wagener swaying on his feet said, "I'll borrow your laser, Stafford. This I want to do for myself."

He forced himself to walk erect, flanked by Stafford and Foden, and marched through the anteroom to his own door. When it slid back, the *Doppelgänger* was still on his feet. But visions of the *hacienda* outside Sao Simao were fading fast. He said, "Too late, gentlemen," and pitched forward on his face on Wagener's long carpet.

Anger flared redly through Mark Chevron's head. It was the last and bitterest twist in a series that had started for him when Paula's laser had cut a swath across his chest. But now the rage was all against himself. He had done it again. This time he was the executioner.

The shoulders under his hands were hyaline as alabaster, but warm. She was not dead or not dead yet.

He twisted her over. Her face was a mask of tears.

She was crying silently, locked in a private world of misery: eyes wide open, unfocused, not seeing him. Chevron said, "Ann. Snap out of it. Listen to me." He shook her like a rag doll, then held her head by two wings of hair, thrust his face centimeters from her own and fairly snarled across the narrow dielectric. "Listen. This is not you. It has nothing to do with you. They slipped the virus into that inoculation. You're not thinking straight. Fight it. Don't be beaten by a gram of chemical crap. You know the techniques."

She was listening, but he was not sure that her data acquisition network was passing it back to the Riley computer. He threw her head to the pillow and raised his hand to smack her face in a memory of shock treatment for hysteria.

Eyes focused suddenly. She was a person and conscious that she was at a disadvantage for receiving a caller. From being a lay figure, she was an individual with a point of view, more important than any mission or vendetta.

Chevron's hands dropped to the pillow on either side of her head. This was at the heart of the matter. The personal link was the key. In spite of experience, in spite of any brainwashing whatever by the system, you had to start there and build from that rock. If the wider commitment did not fit, it had to be rejected. He would stay with her and see her out of this for as long as they might have.

Perception sharpened to an E.S.P. level, she said, "No, Mark. I understand. Do what you have to do. I'll be all right now."

After much voyaging, Chevron recognized he had reached his Ithaca. Lowering his head he docked with gentle precision on her open mouth. It was soft, cool

174

and slightly salty. Slowly her hands moved behind his head, open fingers pushing into his hair.

It was a blank check, a panacea, a starting point for optimism. There was force in the old gag that eros was life. When you had your rock you had to build on it after all. With Kirkegaard he saw that life could only be understood backwards but could only be lived forwards. It was their world and if he knew how to save it, the greatest sin in the book would be not to try.

He moved his lips to her chin, then along the smooth length of her throat to the warm hollow between her breasts. Then he marked the spot with a cross. He said, as though he believed it could be true, "Remember where I was up to. I'm going to talk to Orman. Don't go away, I'll be back."

Before she could answer he had pulled away and was two meters off. "Keep walking about. Go and chat up the natives. I reckon it was a fast-acting dose and you're over the worst."

The old formula sounded strange to his own ears but he used it without qualification as a Párthian shot from the hatch. "Look after yourself. I love you."

He heard her moving and saying, "Mark, wait for me," but he was off down the alley, afraid that resolution would not stand up to any argument.

In the shuttle to Umanaq General, he checked his blaster. The clip was half-empty. Enough remained with careful husbandry for seven lethal charges. Fabiola Dent would do for one. She could take him to Orman. From there he would have to play it by ear. But Southern Hem must have gotten into the very fabric of the complex. He would have to pick his targets with the greatest care.

The same clerk was on duty in reception and looked

surprised to see him. Wonder made an upward spiral when he leaned both hands on her desk and said, "Get that tin-gutted Dr. Dent here but quick."

Reaction was hostile, but not guilty. He judged she was not one of the team.

"What do you want? You have the clearance. Dr. Dent is an extremely busy person."

"She's that all right. Just do it and make it urgent."

"She will not like it."

Chevron's voice was a projection of the cold rage that had taken over in his head. "You won't like it if you don't get your finger out and do it. Just say there is another visitor for clearance. Just that."

Convinced, she selected a sequence on the intercom panel and followed the brief.

"Good. How long will she be?"

"She'll come right over."

"Go and take a coffee break. This is a highly personal interview."

"Who are you?"

Chevron fished out his communicator and showed the seal in his palm. "National Security. Say one word in your coffee bar and I'll have you inside for interrogation."

When she was gone, he went into the inner office and padded round the desk.

There was not much to see. The syringe gun was lying on a sterile pad in the top drawer. It was empty. Special charges would not be left lying about. There were ampules of regular serum neatly labeled and ready for use. Using the special suicide vaccine as freely as they did they would need a supply line.

Beukes. That must have been the Beukes contribution. With free access to every government installation, he was a natural. It was nice to get it straight, if late.

Dr. Dent's quick step made a period. She was through the hatch well before she realized who the visitor was, and then she was on the way out with a good turn of speed in a smooth reverse action.

Chevron beat her to the door and closed it, the blaster lined uncompromisingly on her forehead. He said reasonably, "I expect a mechanical marvel can work without a cog here and there, but I bet you'd miss your brain."

The eyes remained bleak but she stood still. He had hit on a truth. "What do you want?"

"National Security. The jig is up. Tell me about Operation Umanaq."

"Find out for yourself."

"I will. I will." Chevron backed her to the wall behind the desk and opened the drawer. Working with one hand he drew out the syringe gun and thumbed open its butt. Then he looked along the tidy shelf of the dispensary and selected a jar of acetic acid. Depressing a plunger he filled the reservoir and snapped it shut.

"I'm going to start at that turtleneck and work around."

"It won't do you any good."

"That's speculation. Now me, I'm certain sure that it won't do you any good at all."

Extended life span had made her sensitive about the physical facts of living. Also she had developed a knack of reading some way into the mind. It was all true. He was ready to do it. Anxious, even.

"You are too late to halt the operation. An ice age is developing which will devastate the Northern Hemisphere. Unification of the planet under our direction will follow. This is the most far-reaching exercise in sociological engineering that has ever been conceived."

"Take me to Orman."

The eyes were not dead enough to conceal relief. He

177

knew she would do it and believed she could signal ahead what was coming his way. That would be the cyber leg. Micro-circuitry could stack it with every kind of communications gear.

He said, "Take off your coat," and knew he was right.

One emotion was still spilling about in the ironwork. It was hate, refined to a pure essence. But she took it off. "Now the shirt."

Below the neck she was the wrinkled crone of a Witches' Sabbath, a travesty of a human figure mocked by the youthful face above it. But it was there, a light harness and a flat console with a mike diaphragm stuck at the base of the throat.

Nerves crawling with distaste for the chore, he ripped it free and pitched it over the desk.

Then he said equably, "Just put the coat on, it's a warm night. Remember as we go that I'm right behind you and the first shot has your name on it."

It was a fair way. They left the white tiled hospital area and made out into executive country: deep-pile carpets and a long gallery with statuary and strip-lit pictures in heavy gilt frames. It was as incongruous as finding a drawing room at the bottom of a lake. Some head man in the long history of the Polar Complex must have designed it as a proconsular folly. All the chief officers of the complex had a personal suite there.

Orman's baronial outer door was halfway down on the left with an illuminated strip in the paneling: *Medical Director Dr. Franz Orman.*

It was opened by a Latin type nurse with a starched bib full of promise and a comic hat, seconded from the medical coal face for special duty with the top hand. There was another one arranging flowers in the hall. Orman had fixed himself a bonesetter's bunny club.

Dr. Dent, a privileged visitor, said, "I have to see Dr. Orman, Rita. Something urgent has come up."

"In the study, doctor. Shall I call him or will you go through?"

Chevron answered for her, "It's a confidential matter. We'll go to him." Fabiola Dent managed a curt nod of agreement.

Rita operated a wall console and a section of fumed oak paneling rolled silently away. There was a short corridor with subdued, rose-pink strip lighting and an inner barrier of opaque reeded glass which lifted like a portcullis and dropped behind them as they went through.

It was a large room and they had entered it close to one end. Orman was down right, out of the draught, at the end of a ten-meter strip of intense cobalt carpet, sitting at a desk which was built across one corner and partially screened from the rest of the room by a floor divider of pale yellow spars. He was heavily built with a thick pale neck above the stand-up collar of his white tunic. A large, bland, fleshy face turned their way to watch them in. A plump white hand very hairy above the knuckles rested on his right thigh.

His voice was a smooth oily job using a courteous formula, but with a harmonic that left no doubt he was all against being disturbed in the leisure hour.

"Dr. Dent. A pleasure to see you at any time. I do not know this young man, I think."

"This is the man I reported about. He claimed he had a message for you from Dr. Chester."

Orman's reaction was quick but not quick enough. The hand in view was a centimeter from the hidden kneecap when Chevron shot once, a niggardly sparing beam which brought an instant stigmata just below the cuff.

Fabiola Dent saw it as her moment of truth now that

his attention was off her for a spell. She was a meter from a second door close to the angle of the spar screen when Chevron used the remainder of the charge in a bisecting shot down the back of her head.

He did not wait to see which way she fell. Orman was on his feet crossing the gap with a crash start from his cyber leg. For a man of his bulk the speed was uncanny. But Chevron was suddenly seeing the whole set like a sharp-edged still. It was the pay-off, the culmination, the reckoning for Poldano, Zakayo and Paula and some chance of a future for Ann Riley. He was no longer a person, but an instrument and an instrument of destruction at that.

He dropped the blaster and had both hands free to assist the jet-propelled director on his flight path. Orman took off on a low trajectory along his deep blue strip and landed with a jar that would have been the death of any modern apartment.

Chevron was only one second after, diving onto his pneumatic landing mat and finding a comprehensive neck lock before the medico could speak to his leg.

The bull neck took some levering back, but Chevron worked at it, slippery with sweat.

Orman, convinced that his diamond moment of death was suddenly at hand, grated hoarsely, "Wait."

"I've waited a long time. Operation Umanaq is about to have one operator less."

Talking was not easy, but Orman was facing indefinite silence and had a good point to make. "Killing me will not help you. You are too late to alter anything."

"Let me get one thing straight. How is it that the stabilizing gear is not keeping the northern ice cap steady?"

"Once the southern development has begun the load is

too great. Also we have seen to it that the reactors here are not working at full strength."

"That would be noticed."

There was no reply and Chevron increased pressure a fraction.

Orman, turning a nice shade of purple, ground out, "The gauges have been set twenty percent ahead of true reading."

"By whom?"

"The technical director is one of my men."

Chevron recognized that he was destroying a useful property, but he could not afford to leave Orman at his back. Coldly, he applied more power until there was a dry click and the body went slack.

He stood up breathing hard and gathered in his blaster. When he looked again Orman was moving. Ready to fire, he saw the right leg bend from the hip and cleverly juggle with gravity until the body was in balance and standing on it like a sack. Then a siren wail started up. It was telling all that its host had gone out of circuit.

Rita was first through the hatch pulling a bulbous blaster from her bib.

Conserving fire power, Chevron chopped his barrel into the side of her neck and sidestepped as momentum carried her on to cannon into the mobile sack. The leg proved its versatility by hopping about to keep its load in balance without stopping its keening wail.

Chevron reached the street door at a sprint and had it open as the hall began to fill. As he slammed it behind him a quick thinker emptied a clip at the moving wood and the tail end of it burst through the fabric in a narrow tongue that licked into his left shoulder.

The pent-up force of it spun him off his feet. Then he was pounding down the gallery.

181

In the connecting corridor through Umanaq General, Chevron felt that he was beginning to slow up. He overtook a sturdy Malayan nurse driving a dispensing trolley and joined her on its narrow footplate, grabbing her waist with his good arm to find balance.

A girl of quick perception, who prided herself that every crisis found her calm, she said, "The dressing station is at the entrance," and opened the throttle.

"Hold it. All I want is a pad and a sling."

"What you need is a sedative and a bed."

In an imperfect world the just suffer with the unjust. Chevron kicked her foot off of the activator stud and fairly snarled. "Just do as I say. Where's a dressing pack?"

The trolley rolled to a halt. She dropped a leaf in its side and rummaged in a tray, coming out with a gauze slab and a three-cornered bandage.

Chevron had ripped off his shirt and her quick indrawn breath was no boost to morale but she did a quick job.

"Now I'll get a doctor to convince you."

But Chevron had jumped back on the trolley and left her standing open-mouthed. Belatedly she hooked a silver whistle out of her bib and its shrill clamor coincided with the arrival of the posse at the far end of the corridor.

Chevron was already fifty meters off with the trolley rocking on its narrow base and spilling glassware impartially left and right. He skidded to a crash halt and ran through the late Fabiola Dent's office. Outside, an auto shuttle was still waiting for his return trip and he threw himself into the pilot seat.

A diagram of the complex on the console showed that the thermal stabilization plant was on the monorail circuit. He selected the stud and shoved it home, spinning the rheostat for full thrust. The shuttle accelerated away forcing him back for a full due in its deep-sprung squab.

Somewhere he had to make a record. Somebody had to know the score and take it on from where he left off. He flipped open his communicator and said, "Chevron."

Raquel Cunliffe joined him in the cab. "Where are you?"

"Never mind that. Hear this and broadcast it as far as you can. Southern Hem has engineered an ice surge, never mind how. It's likely to blanket most of Europe as far as I can tell. Their communication line runs through the medical service. The crisis is with us now and there may be nothing we can do, but I'm on my way to the stabilization plant in the Polar Scientific Complex. However it goes, a task force should be sent to clean this place up. There's a girl here called Riley. Dr. Ann Riley. She's been a big help. Get that down. I want her looked after. Okay?"

"Mr. Chevron."

"Have you got that?"

"Yes. Now Mr. *Chevron*—"

"Out."

He snapped the case shut, twisted a dial on its outer skin and pitched it out of the shuttle, a brief flare of light through a hurrying shadow ahead. He reckoned he would not be needing it again.

The shuttle was slowing as if followed a long curve left off the main avenue of the underground city and deep into virgin permafrost. It drew up to a long platform with a sentry box and a guard in a heavy parka swinging his arms and carrying a carbine slung over one shoulder.

Chevron took his time climbing out. The sentry, glad of a break, walked energetically to meet him.

"If you want Umanaq General you've missed it. This is a classified area."

"I have to see the technical director."

"Through the arch to the guardroom. State your business there and you'll get an escort if it's important. I still say it's Umanaq General you should be at."

A bleep started up in the sentry box and a yellow light began to flash on its roof. Chevron knew for a truth what the message would be. He fell in behind the guard and was up close as the man leaned in to pick up the handset.

The butt of the blaster thudded into the fur hood and he rocked forward into his box. Chevron reached past him and answered the call.

A voice said urgently, "There's a mental case on the loose. Big man. One arm in a sling. Stop him anyway you like. He has some crazy idea to interfere with the reactors. Warn the director."

"Will do. He won't get past this post."

So the director was on the site. That was good. Chevron, swearing in a monotone at his clumsiness, zipped off the parka and shrugged into it. With his blaster in the right-hand pocket and the carbine over his shoulder he made for the arch.

The guardroom was off left with a long oblong window, partly steamed up. Through it he could see four men playing cards at a low table and one having a solo game at a pin table. As he walked past, keeping a casual pace, one of the card players holding a good hand stuck up a large spatulate thumb in greeting.

Chevron returned it, his face well-shadowed by the hood. Ahead, a broad glistening corridor cut through solid ice bent away to the right. As soon as he was clear of the window he began to run.

Fifty meters on he had to stop with the floor and roof dilating and contracting like a demented throat. He held on to the wall, shoving his forehead against the damp ice until the fit passed. Going on, breathing deeply and talking himself into it, he knew that time was running out.

There was not far to go. He went through a heat-insulating double door into subtropical warmth. The tunnel began to widen and the roof began to slope up. An immense cathedral space had been hollowed out. The road divided left and right in a gallery that circled the well. The floor below was set out like the power house for an immense city: horseshoe computer spreads, consoles, the work heads of reactor pits, too much to take in and evaluate.

Just off center there was a raised command island, a round glass gazebo with two men in white coveralls sitting at a long desk.

Two or three workers on the factory floor raised their heads to look at him, saw nothing remarkable and soldiered on.

He was at the top of a narrow companion leading down when feet pounding in unison sounded from the approach road.

Chevron peeled off his fur, shoved the blaster in his sling, put the carbine strap in his teeth, and went down one-handed. A shout from above signaled the arrival of the guard detail. Faces were turned up to see what it was all about.

At a weaving run, he made for the island.

Men were leaving their desks to close in, but the top hand of the military arm yelled again, "Stand clear. Get away from him."

A single shot rang out to make the point clear and

Chevron heard the whine of an old-fashioned shell centimeters over his head. One-handed he fired his own
carbine up towards the gallery and then threw it away as
the clip emptied.

There was a stampede to get clear. He was isolated
and the guard was on one knee aiming coldly as if on
target practice.

Chevron dived full-length behind a solid console and
found he was sharing it with a small blonde scientist.
Too startled to scream, she was kneeling on all fours with
an open mouth, nervously wetting her lips with a pointed
pink tongue.

Face gray with strain, tunic dark with sweat and
blood, eyes savage, he was no catch to find in her burrow.
When he said, "On your feet, honey and move real slow,"
she followed it to the letter as though mesmerized by a
stoat.

Chevron set the sergeant a problem. He hauled himself up behind and grabbed her around her emotionally
heaving chest with his good arm. In her ear he said,
"Don't worry. It's all in a good cause," and backed slowly
for the island.

There were three steps. He had to lift her to keep a
shield. At the top he was grinding his teeth to keep moving. In spite of assurance, it was a bad sound to hear and
she began to struggle.

Chevron felt the glass swing door at his back, braced
his feet and pushed with his shoulders, letting her go at
the same time. She shot forward down the steps, the
sergeant fired, and Chevron entered the omega point of
his mission in a heap.

The shell sang through the briefly open door and went
into a wild ricochet round the bulletproof dome.

He could not have done better with a designed cover

of fire and movement. The two residents were too busy speculating where it would go next to jump him while he was down. When it gave up its urge on the flank of a memory bin, he was on his feet with the blaster steady in his hand.

Chevron said, "Which one of you two monkeys would be the technical director?"

There was no answer, but unless the printed word told a lie it was the dark one, a lean, stooped character with sideburns and a gold tooth.

Chevron guessed he could not stay long on his feet. He pointed the blaster at the giveaway lapel badge and said, "You are an agent of Southern Hem. You have fixed this installation so that Operation Umanaq can succeed. Thermal injection to stabilize this ice field is below strength."

The other man, thickset, with short wiry hair, was watching his chief for the denial to come. But words were not necessary. It was all true. Surprised and undermined by dodging the hornet ricochet, the director had no time to arrange his face. Instead, he tried to reach a sliding panel on his desktop.

Chevron, fighting double vision, fired until the charge ran out.

He said thickly, "Work out what he's done. You can overrun the maximum on the gauges. Get to it. There's a point of no return coming up."

Knees turning to sponge rubber, the set expanding to a universal blank, he did not know how the transmission went. He did not see the sergeant cross the floor with his section fanned out. Nor did he hear the commotion on the gallery as a whole company of Special Security Commandos deployed from the tunnel and covered the whole area with tripod-mounted lasers.

Henry Wagener using a megavox said curtly, "Anybody who moves a step is a dead man."

Ann Riley said, "Easy, Mark. It's all right. Relax."

Chevron, surfacing from black night and struggling to throw off an immobilizing straight jacket, made no sense of the words. But the tone and the hands on his head carried their own logic.

Her eyes were only centimeters away, very wide under level brows, luminous black milk. Sober, but purged of pessimism. Recall flooded in.

She said again, "It's all right."

He could accept it as an illuminating truth; an anchorage in the eye of the wind which he had never expected to reach. There would be much to do before the situation stabilized, but at a personal level he was home and dry. He said, "We have some unfinished business."

"We fly back tomorrow. In a week you'll be out of your cast. I've been appointed to take charge of your convalescence. There's some talk of giving you a medal."

"It will do to mark the spot better than a notional cross."

"That we shall have to see about in the fullness of time."

Time was as long or as short as you made it. With a newfound patience, he reckoned he could wait as long as it had to be.

The eyes had it. They were affirmative. Whatever the weather in the streets, the subjective climate was set fair.

250774WRL